P9-EGC-666

RATFINK

by

**MARCIA
THORNTON
JONES**

with illustrations by

C.B. DECKER

Dutton Children's Books

An imprint of Penguin Group (USA) Inc.

DUTTON CHILDREN'S BOOKS | *A division of Penguin Young Readers Group*

PUBLISHED BY THE PENGUIN GROUP
Penguin Group (USA) Inc., 375 Hudson Street, New York, New York 10014, U.S.A.
| Penguin Group (Canada), 90 Eglinton Avenue East, Suite 700, Toronto, Ontario M4P
2Y3, Canada (a division of Pearson Penguin Canada Inc.) | Penguin Books Ltd, 80
Strand, London WC2R 0RL, England | Penguin Ireland, 25 St Stephen's Green, Dublin
2, Ireland (a division of Penguin Books Ltd) | Penguin Group (Australia), 250 Camber-
well Road, Camberwell, Victoria 3124, Australia (a division of Pearson Australia Group
Pty Ltd) | Penguin Books India Pvt Ltd, 11 Community Centre, Panchsheel Park, New
Delhi - 110 017, India .| Penguin Group (NZ), 67 Apollo Drive, Rosedale, North Shore
0632, New Zealand (a division of Pearson New Zealand Ltd.) | Penguin Books (South
Africa) (Pty) Ltd, 24 Sturdee Avenue, Rosebank, Johannesburg 2196, South Africa |
Penguin Books Ltd, Registered Offices: 80 Strand, London WC2R 0RL, England

Library of Congress Cataloging-in-Publication Data
Jones, Marcia Thornton.
Ratfink / by Marcia Thornton Jones ; illustrated by C.B. Decker. — 1st ed.
p. cm. Summary: Creative, impulsive Logan vows to turn over a new leaf in fifth grade
so his parents will let him have a pet, but when a competitive new girl arrives at school and
his forgetful and embarrassing grandfather takes over the basement of Logan's house,
doing the right thing becomes harder than it has ever been. ISBN 978-0-525-42066-8
(hardcover) [1. Grandfathers—Fiction. 2. Old age—Fiction. 3. Behavior—Fiction.
4. Conduct of life—Fiction. 5. Schools—Fiction.] I. Decker, C. B., ill. II. Title.
PZ7.J7216Rat 2010 [Fic]—dc22 2009012277

Published in the United States by Dutton Children's Books,
a division of Penguin Young Readers Group
345 Hudson Street, New York, New York 10014
www.penguin.com/youngreaders

DESIGNED BY HEATHER WOOD

Printed in USA | First Edition
1 3 5 7 9 10 8 6 4 2

to katelynn elaine anderson—

may your life be ratfink free!

ACKNOWLEDGMENTS

This book never would have been written

without the extraordinary support of many people

including the best parents ever,

Thelma and Robert Thornton,

the patience and expertise of Steve Meltzer,

the persistence of Susan Cohen

and, of course,

the unending support of my husband, Steve,

who encourages every creative step I take.

RATFINK

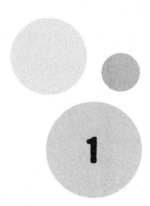

The Naked Truth

Grandpa was naked.

It wasn't as if his doodly-flop was flipping around when I opened the front door. He did have a towel wrapped around his waist. A pink one. With big flowers on it. But the towel didn't quite reach all the way around, so I could tell that underneath Grandpa was absolutely naked.

"He was picking my petunias," Mrs. Spencer said. "Again."

Mrs. Spencer was our neighbor. Before Grandpa

moved in with us, her garden was picture-perfect. That was just a month ago. For some reason, Grandpa thought her flowers were his for the taking, but this was the first time he'd ever gone outside naked to pluck them out of her garden.

Grandpa threw his arms out wide and started singing. Wilted petunias fluttered in his fingers, but that's not what made Mrs. Spencer gasp. It was the fact that his towel slipped. Mrs. Spencer's face had turned as pink as her petunias, and she fanned her face with a blue-veined hand. "Keep him out of my garden," she said, as if I had anything to say about my grandfather's actions. Then she stammered a goodbye and hurried away, although I did notice she glanced once more at Grandpa's sliding towel.

Since moving in with us, my grandfather had done some strange things, but this was by far the absolute worst. "Grandpa," I hissed. "You *cannot* go outside *naked*! What if someone saw you—someone other than a neighbor? Like one of my friends?"

My friends were coming over for a pizza party and easily could have seen my grandfather parading around the neighborhood dressed in a flowery pink towel. The thought of it was enough to make the spit in my mouth turn to cotton. I pushed Grandpa all the way inside, glanced up and down the street one more time to make sure no one else had seen, then slammed the door.

My grandfather hadn't heard a word I'd said, because he was singing too loud. The tune was supposed to be "Mary Had a Little Lamb," but his voice was definitely off-key. "Happy birthday to Charlie! To Charlie! To Charlie! Happy birthday to Charlie! Today's the big one-OH!!!"

I didn't know which was worse. The fact that my grandfather had forgotten to put on clothes or that he had forgotten my name. Again. At least he'd remembered how old I was.

My full name is Charles L. Malone. Middle name Logan. Nobody called me Charlie. Ever. That was Grandpa's name. Even though Mom said I had the same brown eyes and hair that never stayed slicked down, I was nothing like my grandfather.

For one thing, I always wore clothes.

"Logan," I told him, and not for the first time since he moved in with us. "I go by Logan."

Total panic crossed Grandpa's face. He'd only been living with us for four weeks, but I was already used to that look. "Of course," he said. "Logan. I knew that. Now, how about a bowl of cereal, Charlie."

Mom said Grandpa had good days and bad days. This was obviously one of his worst days yet, because he'd also forgotten to put in his dentures.

He had a habit of putting his teeth down and forgetting where they were. Two days ago I'd found them in the geranium Mom kept on the front porch. I hoped he hadn't planted them in my birthday cake.

Grandpa moved fast for an old man. There wasn't anything wrong with his body. It was his mind that gave us all fits. I had to hurry after him when he took off for the kitchen. I looked at the clock over the stove. It was five o'clock in the afternoon. The guys would be here soon.

We had decorated the basement with streamers, and a few of my friends were coming over for pizza and cake. Mom said that was all we could do, since moving Grandpa to our house had taken so much time and energy.

Obviously, Grandpa had forgotten that he'd already had breakfast and lunch, just like he'd forgotten to get dressed.

That's another way I'm different from Grandpa. I never forget.

Grandpa hadn't always been forgetful. He used to work for the government in a top-secret sort of job.

Dad said it wasn't that long ago that Grandpa could add a string of numbers as long as his arm without using a calculator.

Not me. I hate math.

Grandpa rubbed his hands together as if he were trying to keep warm. "Can't wait for your party," he said. "It'll be my first one ever. I'm ready to pin that tail on the donkey!"

The thought of my grandpa wearing nothing but a flowery pink towel and a blindfold in front of all my friends flitted through my brain. Believe me, it was not a pretty sight.

Grandpa gave me a toothless grin and then adjusted the towel, which had slipped dangerously low.

I could not let him ruin the most important birthday ever. It was, after all, the birthday I'd been waiting for since the day my parents had said that when I turned ten I could pick out a pet of my own.

I looked at the clock. The guys would be ringing the bell any minute.

Something had to be done about Grandpa. Fast.

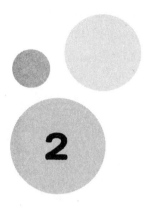

2

Birthday Surprise

"Mom! Dad!" I called into the den without taking my eyes off the gray hair on Grandpa's chest.

No answer.

Since Grandpa had moved in with us, Mom spent a lot of time in the den watching Dr. Phil and Oprah as if they had all the answers.

A naked grandfather was not something a ten-year-old should have to deal with on his very own birthday. I was pretty sure Dr. Phil would agree with me, too.

I knew my parents wouldn't be wrapping my present. There was no way they could wrap up an animal. Besides, they had no idea what kind of pet I wanted. I went to the door of the den.

"MOM!" I yelled. "DAD!"

They stopped talking and smiled at me. "Well, there's the birthday boy," Mom said.

"Are you ready for your party?" Dad asked, checking his watch. "Everyone should be here anytime."

"Exactly. And Grandpa's in the kitchen. Naked," I said. "Mrs. Spencer just brought him to the door. You have to do something."

"Don't you think you're a little old to be telling those stories of yours?" Mom asked.

"Your mother's right," Dad added. "After all, you are ten years old now. You're practically grown up!"

Okay, so I've been known to tell a whopper or two. I couldn't figure out why it was okay to write my tales down and call them a story, but if I said them out loud my parents called them lies. Still, it made me mad that my own parents didn't believe me. "Really," I told them. "Come and see for yourself."

Mom sighed and pushed herself up from the couch. Dad followed her.

Grandpa smiled at them as if nothing was wrong.

"Good morning, Delilah," he said to my mom. "And a glorious morning it is for Charlie's birthday, don't you think?"

My mother's name is Joyce, but she didn't correct him. In fact, she did nothing. She stood, one foot in front of the other, and stared at Grandpa's hairy chest.

When Grandpa first started calling Mom by different names, we just thought he was trying to be funny. It wasn't so funny when he started forgetting other things, like when to take his heart medicine. Then one day he was coming out of the grocery store and couldn't find his car. He wandered around the parking lot so long his ice cream melted. When Dad found out, he decided Grandpa should come and live with us. A month later Grandpa was snoring away in the spare bedroom next to mine.

Mom swiveled on the linoleum, pushed past Dad, and headed back to the den. I followed her. Dad was right behind me.

"Aren't you going to do something?" I pleaded.

"What do you suggest, Logan?" Mom asked.

It was obvious to me. "Maybe make him get dressed? Before someone besides Mrs. Spencer sees him! Someone like my *friends*!"

"Wearing a towel after a shower is not a big thing," Dad said. "He probably did it all the time when he lived alone. Give him time to get used to living with a family again, Logan."

"I don't have time." I pointed to the clock on the wall. "Malik and the guys are going to be here any minute. You have to hide Grandpa before they get here."

"He'll be dressed in time for your pizza party," Mom said. "I promise."

"But we're not hiding anyone," Dad added. "How could you even suggest it?"

"Easy," I said. "If Grandpa ever does something like show up in front of my friends wearing nothing but a pink towel I will never, and I mean *never*, live it down. I'm not taking the chance of my friends finding out that my grandfather is daffy as a duck."

"Logan!" Mom said. "That's not a nice thing to say."

"And he's not crazy," Dad said.

"But he does embarrassing stuff," I said. "Like the time he started singing in the grocery store. And what about burying his dentures in the geranium? Now he's in the kitchen wearing nothing but a towel and waving petunias through the air. If my friends find out about this, I'll be the biggest joke of fifth grade when school starts."

"Kids wouldn't make fun of you because your

grandfather has a little problem," Mom argued.

I looked at Mom. "Don't you remember when you were in fifth grade?" I asked.

I could tell by the look in Mom's eyes that she remembered fifth grade and knew exactly what I was talking about. "Well," Mom said, "they shouldn't."

"Why can't he go live with Uncle Bill instead of us?" I pleaded.

"We've been over this before, Logan. You know your uncle doesn't have room in his tiny New York apartment," Mom said.

"We don't have room, either," I pointed out. Our house was cluttered with stuff. Mom had complained the entire time they were making room for Grandpa in the spare bedroom.

Mom looked at Dad and started talking as if I weren't even in the room.

Mom spoke first: I think we should tell him.

Then Dad: Won't it ruin the surprise?

Mom shrugged: He'll be just as surprised now.

Dad nodded: If you're sure.

"Tell me what?" I nearly shouted.

Mom took a big breath and smiled. It wasn't a real smile, though. It was the kind of smile a nurse gives you right before she jabs you with a needle. "Your father and I thought it over very carefully, and we've decided it's the only way this situation will work."

It's never a good thing when Mom stalls. "Decided what?"

"We're turning the basement into an apartment for your grandfather this weekend," Dad said. "It will be perfect. He'll have a bedroom and his own private sitting room and bathroom. Just think, Logan. No more waking up to find teeth on your sink!"

Grandpa soaked his dentures in a glass by the bathroom sink at night. There was nothing worse than seeing Grandpa's teeth grinning at me through cloudy water the first thing every morning, but that didn't mean I liked the idea of Grandpa taking over the basement—my basement. I wouldn't have been more surprised if my parents had sprouted bat wings and flown away. "But that's where I play Pop-A-Shot and Ping-Pong!"

"We were going to tell you at the party," Mom explained, "but I guess you might as well know now. For your birthday your father and I are going to put shelves in your room. Won't that be nice?"

"Shelves? What kind of birthday present is that?"

"A great one," Dad said, "because we're going to give you your very own television! How's that for a birthday surprise!"

"But . . . but . . . this is my tenth birthday," I said,

the words barely more than a whisper. "You said I could get a pet when I turn ten."

"Oh, Logan," Mom said, and her entire body seemed to sink into the couch. "That's going to have to wait now that your grandfather is staying with us. I just can't handle both."

"But . . . but . . . but . . ."

"Maybe next year," Dad added.

"But you promised," I reminded them.

Mom got up to give me a hug. "I'm sorry, Logan. I know this is your birthday and it isn't what you want to hear, but we all have to make a few sacrifices. After you get used to the idea, you'll be glad to have this opportunity to get to know your grandfather."

"I've got the rest of my life to get to know him," I mumbled.

"But he doesn't," Mom said softly. "Please, Logan. Give this a chance."

"Well, if you ask me, seeing him naked means I'm getting to know him a little too well."

Mom patted my back. "Come on," she said. "You're growing up. Growing up means you're ready to handle some grown-up things—like helping out your family."

I didn't see how a pet had anything to do with

Grandpa. All I knew was that with Grandpa around, any chance I had of playing fetch with Fido had been flushed down the toilet.

Just then the doorbell rang.

I pushed my mom away. "Do something!" I begged. "Before they see him in that stupid towel."

"Don't worry, Logan," Mom said. "You get the door and take your friends straight to the basement. Your father will make sure Grandpa stays put in the kitchen until the coast is clear."

"You have to promise to keep him out of sight," I said.

"I promise, Logan," Mom said without waiting for Dad to decide. "Now go get the door."

As I stomped through the kitchen, Grandpa smiled at me. "Would you mind sliding that cereal box this way, Charlie?" Grandpa asked.

I didn't know what else to do, so I slid my naked grandfather the Cocoa Puffs.

One thing was certain. I had to make sure that nobody, and I mean nobody, found out the truth about Grandpa.

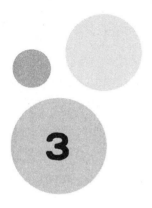

A Surefire Plan

I made it through my party. Mom kept her word. Grandpa stayed up in the guest room while the rest of us ate pizza and played video games. That weekend, Mom and Dad attacked the basement. My stuff was moved out and Grandpa moved in. What didn't fit in my room was stored in the garage. I got my television. It was just a little one, and it wasn't worth telling Malik about. Not that it mattered. I wasn't about to invite him over. Not as long as Grandpa might start singing nursery rhymes and wandering around naked.

Malik had met Grandpa right after he moved in, but I made sure Malik didn't stick around long enough to know Grandpa was one soda pop short of a carton. Nobody knew about Grandpa, and I planned to keep it that way.

I unbuckled my seat belt as Dad pulled up to the curb on the first day of school. I was hoping for a quick getaway. I didn't want any long drawn-out goodbyes. After all, I was in fifth grade now. That's practically middle school. Before I could open the car door, Dad twisted in his seat and reached out to clutch my shoulder. Hard.

"It's a new year, Logan. Let's make it a good one," Dad said.

"That's my plan," I told him. My fingers twitched on the door handle, itching to pull it so I could escape the dreaded father-son talk, but Dad's nails dug into my shoulder, keeping my butt firmly on the seat.

"That's what you've said every year," he said. "But we both know your plans haven't exactly panned out."

"It wasn't my fault the janitor got locked in the girls' bathroom last year," I reminded him. "It was Jake's fault."

My dad closed his eyes, and I saw his lips twitch. I knew what he was doing—counting. It's what he always did when he needed a little patience. I waited until he at least reached ten. "I can't help it if Jake was stupid enough to believe ghosts were haunting the stalls in the girls' room," I said.

"But you were the one that told him the ghost story. And Jake was only in the second grade. You were old enough to know better."

I opened my mouth to argue, but Dad's fingers squeezed my shoulder. "I didn't mean to dig up ancient history today, Logan. My point is that you've had some difficulties in the past. Let's just try not to have a repeat of any of those things, okay?"

"Like I said, Dad, that's my plan."

"Good, so no storytelling. No cheating. No tripping or talking back to the teacher. And no setting other kids up to get in trouble. I want you on your best behavior today and every day for the rest of your life. Got it?"

"Got it," I said. It was easy to agree. I didn't want to spend a minute of fifth grade in detention, and I had a surefire plan guaranteed for success. Instead of getting on the teacher's bad side like I usually did, I was going to become my fifth-grade teacher's best friend. Then I could sail through the year and breeze right into middle school. Dad finally released my shoulder.

I slid out the backseat and slammed the door. The

last thing I saw was Dad giving me a thumbs-up sign before he pulled away from the curb.

I turned and faced Dooley Elementary. Nothing had changed over the summer. It was the same three-story brick building. The same grimy windows. The same chipped steps leading to the double front doors. The only thing different was that it was my last year. I planned to make it a good one.

"Logan! Over here!"

Malik was waiting on the playground near the soccer goals, his backpack sagging halfway down his back. As far as backpacks go, Malik's was nothing special—dark blue with even darker splotches where unknown substances must have been spilled. Probably from some of his backfired science experiments. What made it unique was that ever since last Christmas, Malik never left it out of his sight. It was pretty obvious that he was guarding something important.

I turned, taking off at a trot to join him.

"Watch out!" a shrill voice screamed.

I slammed into a girl who was getting off the bus at that exact minute.

"You should watch where you're going," I told her. She was tall. Like me. I could look straight into her blue eyes.

"Me? Look what you did!" she yelped.

I looked at the ground where she was pointing. "What?" I asked.

"You messed up my shoes," she said. She squatted down and started swiping at a smudge.

"There's nothing wrong with your shoes," I said. "It's just a little dirt."

The girl looked up at me, her eyes squinting in a frown. "They're brand-new," she said. "I just got them yesterday, but now, thanks to you, they're all dirty."

I didn't get the big deal over a bit of dirt, but I could tell she was upset. "Gee," I said, "I'm sorry. Are you new here?"

The girl stood up and tossed her blond hair over her shoulders. Everything about her matched, from the blue edging of her socks to the blue barrette in her hair. It looked like her tennis shoes weren't the only new things she had. There was a price tag hanging from the neck of her blue-striped shirt. When I reached over and snapped it off, the tips of her ears turned red. I knew the feeling. My ears did the same thing when I was embarrassed. I handed her the tag.

"I'm Logan. Fifth grade."

"My name is Emily. Emily Scott. I'm in fifth grade, too."

"Maybe we'll be in the same class," I told her.

"Look at Logan," someone yelled. "He has a girl-friend."

I could feel my own ears starting to burn and had a sneaking suspicion they were turning bright red, too. "I do not," I yelled automatically.

I turned, looking for the body that went with the voice. I didn't have to look far to find Justin. He and Randy were coming up the walk, backpacks slung over their shoulders. I gave Justin a shove. "Take it back," I said, but he only laughed and shoved me back. Which, of course, caused me to step on Emily's other shoe.

"Sheesh," she said, hopping away. "I told you my shoes were new." And then Emily Scott marched away.

"Who was that?" Randy asked.

"A new girl," I said without thinking. "Emily. Emily, the Snot, Scott. Whatever you do, stay away from her shoes!"

Malik walked up, his backpack even lower on his shoulder. An assortment of key chains dangling from the zipper pulls on the outside pockets jangled when he walked. Whenever he visited his dad, he came home with a few more key chains decorating his pack. There was something important in that pack, and I wanted to know what it was. Who wouldn't? Every day I tried a new guess. I'd already tried the obvious stuff like baseball cards, spy secrets, and pirate treasures.

"I know," I said as Malik slid his backpack down his arm. It thumped to the ground by his sneakers. I noticed one of his socks was red and one was purple. "It's the mummified remains of King Tut's hamster," I guessed.

Malik looked at me and blinked three times. Blink, blink. Blink. That's what he always did when he was confused, and I tended to confuse him a lot.

"In your backpack," I said. "Is that what's in there? A tiny wrinkled mummy?"

Malik stopped blinking and rolled his eyes instead. "Wrong again," he told me.

"Come on," Randy said. "You can tell us. We'll never rat you out."

Malik hiccuped. He always hiccuped when he was embarrassed. "I know you won't," Malik told them, "because you'll never know."

Just then the bell rang. "Hurry," I said, pushing Malik toward the door. "I have to get to class."

Justin and Randy stopped dead in their tracks. "Are you sick?" Randy asked.

"Okay. So I don't have a stellar reputation as a

student. But things are about to change," I said as I rushed up the steps and through the front doors to Dooley Elementary. I explained my plan as we went. "I'm going to get in good with the teacher right from the start. Then it'll be smooth sailing for the rest of the year."

Justin laughed. "You? A teacher's pet? That'll never happen."

I was about to argue when the principal, Mrs. Hollis, stepped out of her office. Hollis the Hawk and I knew each other . . . too well. "Logan," she said when she saw me. "Come with me."

"What did I do?" I yelped.

"Nothing. I hope," she said. "I need your help." Mrs. Hollis had a habit of looking at kids from over the top of her glasses. When she did that it made her look like a hawk. I was the one that had come up with the nickname of Hollis the Hawk; hopefully she didn't know that.

"I need to get to class," I said.

"Don't worry, you'll get there."

There was no arguing with Hollis the Hawk. I heard Justin and Randy laughing as they followed Malik down the hall.

I did a double take when I saw who was in the office. The new girl. Emily. I couldn't believe she had come straight to the principal's office to rat me out just because of a little smudge on her sneakers. "I didn't mean it," I blurted. "It was an accident. Really."

Mrs. Hollis looked at me from over the top of her glasses. "Didn't mean what, Mr. Malone?"

I looked at Emily. She stood with her arms crossed and gave a tiny shake of her head. "Nothing?" I squeaked.

Mrs. Hollis looked from me to Emily and back to me again. "I can't believe the first day of school hasn't even begun and you're already stirring up trouble. Let's not have a repeat of last year, Logan."

"Okay. I mean no. I mean no there won't be a repeat," I stuttered. I couldn't help but hear Emily's little snicker. The new girl obviously enjoyed watching me squirm.

"Good," Mrs. Hollis said. "The reason I called you into the office was that I need you to show Miss Scott to her classroom. I trust you can be a gentleman and help her get acquainted with Dooley Elementary. Let me just finish up some paperwork and then you two can be on your way."

How could I refuse? The late bell rang, and Mrs. Hollis had us sit while she made morning announcements and recited the Pledge of Allegiance. Then we waited while two third graders stumbled over reading what glop the cafeteria planned to serve. Finally, Mrs. Hollis was able to make Emily an official student at Dooley Elementary, and she sent us on our way.

The halls were quiet when the door to the office shut behind us. "I can't believe you made me late for the first day of class," I huffed at her.

"I can't believe you thought I'd tattle on you for stepping on my shoes," she huffed right back.

"Well, I'm glad you didn't. Thanks for that . . . at least."

"Why are you in such a hurry, anyway?" she asked.

I could hardly tell the new girl my secret plan for staying out of trouble. After all, I didn't want her to think I *wanted* to be a teacher's pet. So I did what I do best. I call it fiction; my parents call it lying. Whatever it was, I was good at it. I pulled Emily close and whispered, "I need to sit near the front so I can see the board because I have this rare eye condition. When the light shines in at a certain angle, my brain hiccups and changes real life into images of blobs and monsters and things so scary they could give you nightmares for life. But if I sit close, I can concentrate on bending the light back. It's sort of like a reverse laser power. There are only a few people in the world able to do it. I had to have special training and every-thing, but I have to be close to the front of the room to do it."

"Wow," Emily said. "I've never heard of anything like that before."

I smiled at how gullible the new girl was. "I try to keep it a secret, so don't tell anyone, okay?"

I didn't wait to hear anything else Emily had to say. We hurried down to the fifth-grade wing. Our new classroom was all the way at the end of the hallway. "Wait," Emily said before I opened the door. "Do you think I look okay?" she asked. "Is my hair messed up?"

"Who cares?" I asked. I was already getting tired of Emily Scott and I was ready to shove her aside, but then I looked at her face. The blood had drained from her cheeks, and she bit the inside of her lower lip. I recognized that look because I had seen it a dozen times on my grandfather's face. It was fear. "Don't worry," I told her. "This will be a breeze."

And then I opened the door to the fifth grade.

Mr. Simon stopped in midsentence and looked at me as if I had just barfed all over his lesson plans.

"We have an excuse," I said in a rush, and handed him the note from Mrs. Hollis. Mr. Simon glanced at me and then read the note. When he looked up at Emily his face melted in a smile. "Class, I would like everyone to meet a new student. Emily Scott. Please pick a seat," he told her.

Emily and I looked at our options. There were only two empty desks left in the room. One right next to Mr. Simon's desk and one in the next row. Which wouldn't be bad for implementing my plan except that the second seat was right behind Monster Mooney's desk. Monster Mooney just happened to be as big as a professional football player. Mr. Simon wouldn't even know I existed if I had to sit behind him. I sighed and started around Monster.

"I'll take that seat," Emily said. When I looked at her she gave me a little smile. "You can have the other one," she said as she passed me.

I couldn't believe it. Maybe, just maybe, Emily Scott wouldn't be so bad after all.

4

A Winning Strategy

That afternoon Coach York finished gym class with four-person relay races. I was on the same team as Justin, Randy, and Rachel. I would never say it out loud, but I was glad Malik was on the new girl's team. Don't get me wrong. Malik and I are best friends, but he isn't a fast runner, and everyone knows that the whole point of running a relay is to win.

Emily Scott took one look at Malik and laughed. "You can't run a race with that," she said, pointing at Malik's backpack sagging from his left shoulder.

Blink, blink. Blink. "Yes, I can," Malik told her.

"Are you nuts?" she said. "That thing looks like it's full of bricks. It'll weigh you down. Our team will lose for sure. And I hate to lose."

"Don't let her push you around," Justin told Malik.

"That's right," I added. "You can do what you want."

Which is exactly what Malik did. Emily stared at Malik, her mouth hanging open in total disbelief, as he lined up to race with his backpack hanging on his back. At least he put both straps on his shoulders so it didn't make him lopsided.

I wasn't about to admit I thought Emily might be right. Like I said, a race is all about winning, but Malik was on the other team so I didn't tell him that.

Justin pulled my arm to bring me into my team's huddle. "Forget about Malik. We have a race to win and I have a plan. Logan will run last."

"I always go last," Rachel said. "I'm the fastest."

Justin pointed at my feet. "Logan's legs have grown since last summer. I'm betting he's faster now," he said.

I looked over at the new girl. She was at least a head taller than Malik. I tried to make my back straighter, but that made me think about how Grandpa always stood as if he had a pole stuck down his pants, so I let my shoulders slump again.

Coach York blew his whistle, and I had to make a mad dash to get in place on the track.

We lined up. Ready to run. Coach York blew the whistle again, and runners sprinted onto the track. Rachel ran first for our team. Her legs were a blur as she rounded the corner.

The new girl was obviously right about one thing. Malik's backpack slowed him down. Way down . . . which was good for us. Malik lost a lot of ground for his team.

We were ahead. Justin lost some ground, but as he turned the corner and headed for me we were still in the lead.

I faced front, holding my hand back, ready for the baton. SLAP! I had it.

I dug my sneakers into the track and took off. I heard the rest of the class scream as I aimed for the finish line. I risked a glance over my shoulder. There was only one person gaining on me.

Emily.

I ducked my head. I pumped my arms. Still, I heard Emily's super-white sneakers slapping the ground right behind me. One thing was for sure, the new girl could run. Fast.

We were neck and neck. The finish line was just ahead, but I was going to do it. I was going to beat Emily Scott!

And that's what would have happened if I hadn't tripped on my loose shoestring at that exact moment. Down I went in a tumbling cyclone of legs and arms and feet.

Unfortunately, I took down Emily Scott, too.

Randy jumped over us and breezed past the finish line. Next came Bobby and Sharissa.

Emily and I lay on the ground, a tangled knot in the middle of the track. The rest of the class gathered around us, laughing as if we were funnier than circus clowns.

"You did that on purpose," Emily snapped. "You and Malik with his stupid backpack planned this just to make me look like an idiot."

I hadn't, but it would have been a good strategy, and a grin slipped across my face.

"You," Emily hissed in my ear like a poisonous snake, "are dead meat!"

Logan the Liar

It was before lunch on Friday when Emily Scott struck back. A bunch of girls were clustered around Emily as if she were some sort of rock star. Malik and I tried to make our way around them, and we were almost to the water fountains when Emily's voice stopped us.

"What's the deal with that backpack?" she asked Malik.

Malik was the only kid at Dooley who took his backpack to lunch. He paused, blinking three times, and automatically leaned to the right to balance the

load. Malik had carried his pack for so long I wondered if he would know how to stand straight without
it slung on one side or the other.

"Ignore her," I said and kept going.

Emily pushed through the group of kids and walked
up to Malik to tug on his backpack. "What do you
keep in there?" she asked. "You've carried it around
all week long like it's something special. Thanks to
your backpack, we even lost our race and you made
me look like a fool. So tell me. What's inside?"

"You'll never get him to tell," Sharissa said.

"We've been trying to see inside for months," Barbara added.

"Is it love letters to your babysitter?" Emily asked.

Sharissa and Barbara giggled. I hate girlie giggles.

Emily tossed her shoulders back and smiled at the
girls surrounding her. I remembered how Emily had
looked before we went in the classroom on the first
day of school. She had been scared. Not anymore.
Now she acted as if she were the leader of a pack of
werewolves.

"Is it your teddy bear?" she asked, tugging harder
on Malik's backpack.

Something about the way Emily enjoyed the laughs
of the people around her made me think of Grandpa.

I'd seen him puff out his chest and stand tall when he was trying to make people forget that he'd done something stupid.

"I know," Emily said. "I bet it's an extra pair of underwear in case you wet your pants."

Barbara's face turned red at the word *underwear*, but Sharissa laughed so hard she snorted. So did a few other kids hanging out near the door. That seemed to make Emily stand even taller.

I couldn't believe how the new girl had turned as vicious as a rabid pit bull. Malik had been my best friend since, well, since forever. I knew for a fact that Malik wouldn't stand up for himself. It wasn't fair the way she kept making fun of him just so she could get a few giggles out of the other kids. I couldn't let her keep picking on him.

"Leave him alone," I said.

Emily faced me. "Who do you think you are?" she asked. "His bodyguard?"

Obviously, Emily Scott wasn't the kind of kid to back down from anything or anybody. Neither was I.

"As a matter of fact," I said slowly, "I am."

"Oh, no," groaned Justin.

"Don't get him started," Rachel warned. She rolled her eyes so hard I was afraid they might get stuck.

I ignored them both.

"What you don't know," I said, "is that Malik is the exiled son of an empire's ruler. It's a small empire, but it's one of the richest in the world."

"Here he goes," Justin said.

"Logan is famous for his stories," Sharissa told Emily.

"There's no stopping Logan once he gets started," Barbara added with a grin. I liked the way the crowd was facing me now, instead of Emily, making me center stage.

The words rose up inside me like a burp after chugging soda pop. "His country is so rich all the toilets are made of gold," I told the new girl. "Teachers drive sports cars, and kids don't have to do their own homework because they all have personal tutors."

I was on a roll, but Emily didn't like the way everyone was suddenly paying more attention to me. I could tell by the way she put her hands on her hips and glanced around the circle of faces.

"That's just another lie," Emily interrupted. "Like the one you told me about your eyes turning shadows into monsters."

Obviously, she had finally figured out that the eye condition I told her about on the first day of school was just a story. It had taken her long enough, which proved to me she wasn't the brightest lightbulb in the hallway, but I didn't tell her that. Instead, I said innocently, "This is no lie, but I understand why you wouldn't believe me. After all, I'm sure *you* haven't heard about it. You have to be super-smart to know about his empire."

"Zing," Justin said.

"Ouch," Rachel added.

Maybe I had crossed a line. It didn't sound very nice even to my own ears. But it was too late to take back the words. They were already out of my mouth, hanging in the air between the new girl and me. I could tell Emily thought the same thing. Everyone was waiting to see what she would do next. Even me. Her entire future at Dooley Elementary depended on it.

Emily took a step in my direction. "Big words from Logan the Liar," she said, pointing a finger dangerously close to my chest. "But I am smart. Smarter than you and smarter than Malik with his backpack. Just wait and see. I'll teach you to make me look stupid in front of everyone."

And then Emily pushed past me on her way into the cafeteria. Unfortunately, when she shoved me out of her way, I stumbled right through the door into

the girls' bathroom. That's when I discovered there is something way more terrible than girlie giggles.

Shrieks.

"I can't believe you went into the girls' bathroom," Justin said later that afternoon as soon as Coach York looked away.

"I didn't go in there," I said for at least the millionth time. "I was pushed. By Emily."

Ever since lunch, I had been explaining to all my friends how I had ended up in the girls' room. No matter how many times I said it, no one would believe that I hadn't gone in on purpose. Not even Mr. Simon.

Did Emily apologize? Nope. She laughed louder than everyone else. Proof positive that sweet little Emily Scott wasn't so sweet at all. And now I knew how it was going to be. When it came to being a friend or foe, Emily was the biggest foe of all.

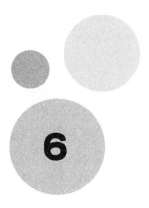

6

Trouble Times Seven

Plop.

The tiny piece of paper landed smack-dab in the middle of my desk. There was only one place that wad could have come from. I glanced across the aisle. Emily stuck out her tongue at me. I was getting used to the sight. Since I had knocked down Emily two weeks earlier, she had made it her life's mission to make me miserable.

Well, she could throw a thousand wads of paper and stick out her tongue clear to her knees. I wasn't going to let her bother me.

For some reason, my fifth-grade teacher had this insane idea that we should be able to complete an entire page of math facts in less than three minutes. He started every class with a timed test. I couldn't figure out how Emily had time to make spitballs and do the timed math test when it took me an entire minute just to get through the first row. I was definitely not like my grandfather. On a good day he would be able to finish a timed multiplication test so fast it would make Mr. Simon's head spin. I imagined my teacher's head spinning in a flushing toilet. I couldn't help but smile.

"Logan," Mr. Simon said. "Eyes on your own paper."

Sharissa and Barbara glanced up from their papers and giggled.

That brought me back to reality. "I wasn't copying," I told him.

Mr. Simon pressed his lips in a tight line and looked at me over the top of his glasses. "Save your stories for your journal, Logan," Mr. Simon said.

I felt the tips of my ears burn. I already knew Mr. Simon well enough to tell he was in no mood to argue. I kept my mouth shut.

I figured Emily Scott was grinning, but I didn't give her the satisfaction of glancing her way. I looked down at the numbers swimming across my math paper. The seven times table was the absolute hardest.

Plop.

Another spitball landed in the middle of my math paper. I flicked it to the floor without looking up. No need to. I knew who had sent it flying. Emily.

Plop.

Plop.

Two more soggy wads of paper landed on my desk. I sighed and glanced at Emily without thinking. She grinned and crossed her eyes. Personally, I hoped her face got stuck like that. Then Mr. Simon would see that the real Emily Scott wasn't the blond-haired, freckle-faced, smiling teacher-pleaser she pretended to be. She was actually a stick-her-tongue-out-and-trip-you-in-the-hallway kind of troublemaker. If you asked me, Emily should have been on our math test. She was trouble times seven.

The egg timer on Mr. Simon's desk was ticking away. Everyone else in the room was rushing to scribble answers. Malik was probably checking his by now. I knew for a fact that he was determined to get more right than Emily.

I was only on the second row. It shouldn't have been so hard. After all, Grandpa had tried to help me the night before. He had sung the multiplication tables to the tune of "Twinkle, Twinkle, Little Star" all the way to fifteen times fifteen in that deep, off-key voice of his.

Having your grandfather sing to you was not something a kid who was almost in middle school would ever admit to. The sound of his voice rambled through my head half the night. I thought it would give me nightmares.

For some reason, whenever Mr. Simon started that timer, my brain went totally blank. It was as if the tick-tick-tick of the timer crowded out everything else in my brain. I wondered if that's how Grandpa felt when he was trying to remember my name.

I skipped seven times six and tried seven times eight. I didn't know that, either. At the rate I was going, I would be known as the dumbest math kid ever to go to middle school. I reached down to scratch the bottom of my foot when Emily slid from her seat.

Usually, Mr. Simon didn't let anybody out of their seats during a timed math test. Of course, Emily wasn't just anybody. She smiled sweetly, fluttered her eyelashes, and held up her pencil so he could see the broken point. Mr. Simon smiled back and nodded knowingly, as if he and Emily were passing secret spy messages by code.

I went back to my math as Emily strolled past me on her way to the pencil sharpener.

Tick-tick-tick. The timer was counting down to zero.

I focused on seven times five, trying to count it out in my head.

Tick-tick-tick.

I ignored the whirring pencil sharpener and wrote thirty-two. That didn't look right. I erased the two and wrote a four. That looked a little better, but I still had a feeling that it was wrong.

Tick-tick-tick.

I was getting ready to erase the four when Emily passed me on the way back to her desk. That's the exact moment that Emily Scott jabbed me right in my leg with her just-sharpened pencil.

Now, who could blame a kid for jumping up from his seat and screaming bloody murder when something like that happened?

Simon Says

Dad and Mom were waiting at the kitchen table the next morning. Usually Dad was long gone for work by the time I wandered in for breakfast. Today they both looked up when I walked into the kitchen, as if they had been waiting hours just for me.

"Comb your hair, Logan," Dad said. I spit on my hand and smoothed it across the spot right over my forehead where my hair always stuck up. It stayed down for three seconds before I felt it spring back up again.

It didn't help when Grandpa walked up behind me and roughed up my head as if he were rubbing a balloon to make static electricity. "Anybody seen my chompers lately?" he asked.

I glanced at Grandpa to make sure he was dressed. He was, but his teeth were not in his mouth.

We all jumped into action. Dad left the kitchen to look in the living room. Mom went to look in the den. I searched through the kitchen drawers and cabinets. Grandpa poured a cup of coffee and sat at the table as if nothing was wrong at all. I sighed and opened the refrigerator. There they were, stuck right in the middle of the butter dish.

"Found 'em!" I yelled loud enough for Mom and Dad to hear.

"Yep, that's them," Grandpa said as he plucked his dentures from the butter dish and slipped them in his mouth. He didn't even bother washing the butter off. "Thanks, Charlie. You're one heck of a grandson."

"Logan," I said without thinking as I dumped the stick of butter into the garbage. "I'm Logan."

That confused look passed across Grandpa's face. "Right," he said as Mom and Dad came back into the room. "Logan. How about you and me shooting some baskets this afternoon?" he asked. "I'll meet you at school and we can walk to the park together."

"NO!" I blurted a little too quickly. Since moving my Pop-A-Shot from the basement to the garage, Grandpa had shown me that he still had some moves. It was okay shooting baskets with him in the garage, but that didn't mean I wanted to do it in public. Grandpa might sound perfectly normal, but I knew the real truth. With my luck, he would show up at school wearing a tutu and flowers in his hair. Everyone would find out he was nuttier than peanut butter and nobody would laugh harder than Emily Scott.

"I think it's a great idea," Mom said as she came back into the room. "Then I can run to the mall and do some shopping." Mom used to work at a dentist's office, but when Grandpa moved in she gave up her job. She said it was to help him get settled, but I knew the truth. It was to make sure Grandpa stayed out of trouble.

"I'll come home," I told him. "Then we'll shoot some baskets in the garage. Do *not* come to my school."

I looked away from Grandpa's eyes. I didn't like the hurt I saw behind the confusion, but then he seemed to forget about everything. He picked up a mug, poured in coffee, and squirted pancake syrup into it as if that was the most normal thing in the world to do. My stomach did a flip-flop just smelling the syrup and coffee mixed together. Then he reached in his shirt pocket and pulled out five pink packets of sweetener.

"Where did you get those?" Mom asked.

Grandpa looked at the packets in his hand. That where-in-the-world-did-you-come-from look crossed his eyes again.

Lately, Grandpa had been showing up with all sorts of strange things. Sugar packets, toothbrushes, packages of M&M's. I was pretty sure he wasn't paying for any of them, but I wasn't about to say a word.

Dad glanced at Mom and gave a little shake of his head. "Not now," he mouthed.

Mom closed her eyes for a brief second and took a deep breath. Then she put her hand on Grandpa's arm. "Forget about the sweetener, Pops. We need to talk to Logan for a few minutes."

Grandpa looked at Mom. "Go right ahead, Clementine," he said, and reached for the cereal box. "Talking doesn't bother me a bit!"

"Joyce," Dad said. "Her name is Joyce. And she meant alone. We need to talk to Logan in private. Why don't you take your coffee into the den?"

Grandpa smiled and gave me a wink.

"I see a little trouble in your future," he said as he ruffled my hair again. "I'll get out of the way before the bullets start to fly." He whistled a tuneless song and left the kitchen.

Dad waited until Grandpa was gone. "Have a seat, Logan," he said. "We need to talk."

When Dad says those words he isn't interested in talking about basketball. It means I'm in trouble. "I don't have time," I said. "I'll be late for school."

"I'll drop you off on my way to work," Dad offered. "Sit."

"Then *you'll* be late," I said, trying to be helpful. Dad worked in an accounting office. He was good with numbers just like Grandpa.

"I already called the office," Dad said.

What choice did I have? I sat.

"I'm glad you're getting along with your grandfather," he said. "It's a big help to your mother when you spend time with him."

I let out a whoosh of air. Here I thought I was in big trouble, but Dad was actually complimenting me. "Grandpa's okay as long as he doesn't act weird in front of my friends," I said honestly.

"There is no need to be embarrassed, Logan," Mom said. "He can't help it if he's different from most people. He's unique. Just like you are."

"I am *not* like Grandpa," I blurted.

Dad ignored what I'd said. "Your mother is right. Grandpa has always been a character. It's just more . . . er . . . pronounced now that he's getting . . . um . . . older. We're proud of how responsible you've been since he's come to live with us. You really shouldn't keep hiding him from your friends."

I tried to argue around a mouthful of Frosted Mini-Wheats, but milk squirted from between my two front teeth. Mom handed me a napkin.

"Now, we need you to act just as responsible at school," Mom said as I mopped up the milk.

"I am responsible," I mumbled through my cereal, but it sounded more like "M reshponshbul."

"Don't talk with your mouth full," Dad reminded me.

And then the entire conversation took a turn so sudden I almost spit out cereal sludge.

"Mr. Simon called last night," Mom said. "He wanted to talk about your behavior."

"Again," Dad added.

Mr. Simon wasn't the least bit like my fourth-grade teacher. She had pretended I didn't exist. Not Mr. Simon. He watched every breath I took, just waiting for me to hiccup. When I did, he called my parents. I was pretty sure he had our number on speed dial.

"I'm good," I told my parents. "Really I am."

"We know you're a good kid, but telling lies is not what Mr. Simon calls being good," Dad said.

"I don't lie," I said.

Dad looked me straight in the eyes. "What about Monday's homework?"

He had me there. On Sunday night Grandpa had challenged me to a contest. We stood at my open bedroom window and sailed paper airplanes across the yard to see whose went farthest. I thought it was a great idea until I realized he was using my math homework for planes. By the time I figured it out it was too late. My homework was ruined and I didn't have time to do it over. Obviously, I couldn't tell Mr. Simon the truth in front of the entire class. So I did what I do best.

I didn't really expect Mr. Simon to believe a vampire bat had flown into my room at midnight and pooped all over my papers, but the class thought it was one of my best stories. They laughed so hard Bobby fell out of his chair and Rachel started choking. Mr. Simon, however, did not think it was very funny. He had called Mom less than an hour later.

"It was a joke," I argued. "I wasn't really lying."

"You weren't telling the truth, either," Dad pointed out.

"You're getting too old to tell stories," Mom added.

"Writers do it all the time," I told her. "How come it's okay to write a story but it's not okay to tell one?"

Dad closed his eyes. He took a deep breath and then looked at me again. "Mr. Simon did not call this time about your math homework," he continued. Even though it was early in the morning, my dad's voice sounded very tired. "It was about yesterday. Your teacher did not appreciate when you stood up in the middle of math class and screamed."

I may not be the smartest kid at Dooley Elementary, but I'm not exactly dumb. I could see why a teacher would complain about screaming kids if he didn't know the whole story. I had tried to tell Mr. Simon what really happened, but he'd actually rolled his eyes when I said Emily stabbed me. Whenever I rolled my eyes I got yelled at, but I knew better than to point that out to Mr. Simon.

"Lying will get you nowhere in my class. Mr. Malone," Mr. Simon had said. He always called kids by their last names when he was mad.

I tried to tell him it was the absolute truth, but Mr. Simon wouldn't listen. Instead, he had called Mom and Dad. Again.

If anyone should listen to kids it should be their parents. Right? "It wasn't my fault," I tried to explain.

Dad held up his hand as if he were stopping traffic. "Did you stand up in math class yesterday?" Dad asked.

"Yes, but—"

"And did you let out a bloodcurdling scream?" he wanted to know.

"Yes, but—"

"And," Dad went on, "did your behavior cause the rest of the class to stop working on their timed multiplication test?"

"Yes, but Emily—"

Dad's hand flew up again, a shield stopping my words in midair.

"This has nothing to do with Emily," Dad said.

That just shows how wrong parents can be. This had everything to do with Emily. Since I had accidentally knocked her down she had been dreaming up ways to get me in trouble. That was the truth and nothing but the truth, but did Dad let me tell it?

Nope.

"No more stories, Logan," Mom said. "Mr. Simon says you have to try harder, and we agree with him. You're in fifth grade. Next year you start middle school. It's time you stop causing problems in class and act responsibly."

"Simon says this, Simon says that," I muttered under my breath. Mom and Dad pretended they didn't hear, which was probably a very good thing.

Dad stretched over to tug my agenda from the stack of books piled on the counter. Our agendas were spiral notebooks with a column for each day of the week where we wrote our assignments. At the bottom of the page was a small blank space for notes. Dad flipped my agenda open and jabbed his finger at the bottom of a column.

"Mr. Simon is going to watch you like a hawk," Dad said.

"More like a buzzard," I mumbled.

Dad closed his eyes again and counted. I was beginning to hope the worst of this conversation was over until Dad opened his eyes and told me the rest of Mr. Simon's diabolical plan. "We're keeping it simple. If you make it through the day without getting into trouble, Mr. Simon will draw a smiley face at the bottom of the day's column. If you start telling tall tales again, it will be a frowny face."

Dad slipped a pen from his shirt pocket and drew a circle on the page just inside the cover of my agenda notebook. He added two eyes and a giant smile in the center. "This is to remind you. *Be good.*"

I slumped down in my chair and stared at the picture my dad had drawn. "Who cares?" I muttered. "Smiley faces are for kindergartners."

"*You* should care," Mom told me, "because your father and I are making you a deal. If you bring home two weeks' worth of smiley faces, we're going to let you get what you've been begging for."

I sat up straighter in my chair and looked hard at Mom. "You mean it?" I asked. "I can join the circus and become a lion tamer?"

Mom nearly spit out a mouthful of coffee. "Where do you get these ideas?" she asked. "Of course you're not joining the circus."

I slid down in my chair. "Then what do I get?"

Dad crossed his heart and held up two fingers in a Malone family pledge. "We promise that if you bring home good reports for the next two weeks, we will let you get a pet of your very own. Cross my heart and hope for pie!"

That's what my family always said when we were promising something big, because Mom said it was stupid to hope to die.

"You said I couldn't have a pet because Grandpa moved in," I reminded them.

Dad let Mom answer. "I was wrong. It's not fair of us to ask you to put your life on hold," she said. "Your father and I talked it over last night. Every boy should have a pet, but you have to prove you're ready for the responsibility. That's the deal."

"And once you get a pet, it's up to you to take care of it," Dad added.

For the first time that morning I grinned. "I can have any pet that I want?" I asked. "Even if it's a snake?"

Mom's lips pressed into a straight line, and I thought that maybe, just maybe, I should have kept the snake idea to myself.

"Can you do it, Logan?" Dad asked, totally ignoring what I'd said about a snake. "Can you be good for two weeks straight—ten whole days in a row?"

Now it was my turn to make a promise. "Mr. Simon won't even know I'm in the room!" I told Dad. "Cross my heart and hope for pie!"

8

Emily, the Snot, Scott

Malik was waiting for me on the soccer field. He let his backpack slip to the ground. It landed with a dull thump.

"What took you so long?" Malik asked. "We're going to be late."

Malik actually looked forward to school. The idea of science projects was more exciting to him than Christmas morning, and I'm pretty sure he thought Mr. Simon's timed math tests were better than running relays in gym class.

"My family," I told him.

"You're so lucky," Malik said.

I nearly choked on the word. "Lucky?"

When Malik nodded, his glasses slid halfway down his nose again. "Getting to have breakfast with your mom and dad. Now even your grandfather is there."

Ever since his dad moved out, Malik had this mistaken idea that everyone else's family was better. He actually thought having my grandfather move in was a good thing. If only he knew the truth.

"I wasn't late because we were having a party at breakfast," I said. "I was late because Mr. Simon called my house. Again."

Blink, blink. Blink. Malik's eyelids fluttered. Obviously he had no idea what I was talking about. "Remember yesterday?" I asked. "When Emily, the Snot, Scott stabbed me with her pencil?"

Malik nodded, but I could tell he still didn't get it.

"Well, Mr. Simon blamed *me* for that," I explained so Malik wouldn't get a headache from all that blinking. Then I told Malik about the deal my parents had made. I finished by showing him the stupid cartoon face on the page inside the cover of my agenda.

"Can you believe it?" I sputtered. "Smiley faces! I'm trying to get ready for middle school and my parents are treating me like I'm in kindergarten!"

"Maybe it won't be so bad," Malik said. That's the kind of friend he was. No matter how awful things seemed, he always tried to make me feel better. "Just get through two weeks and then it'll be over. Besides, hippies in the 1960s put smiley faces on everything. And a lot of them were teenagers."

"Where do you learn that stuff?" I asked.

"The History Channel," he said, as if it were as normal as watching the Red Sox in the World Series. Malik watched the History Channel instead of cartoons and the Discovery Channel instead of ESPN.

"Don't you ever get tired of learning stuff?" I asked.

"Never. I'm going to be the smartest kid to breeze through middle school honors classes." Malik hoisted his backpack and slung it over his right shoulder, and we headed toward school.

"You really should clean that thing out," I told Malik when he veered to the right to balance the load in his pack and bumped into me. "It's a hazard to your health, and depending on what you have hidden in there, everyone else's, too. Hey! You wouldn't happen to have a cure for Emily Scott hidden in there, would you?"

Malik shifted his pack to the other shoulder, which

made him lean a little to the left. "There is no cure
for her. She's worse than the bubonic plague. Your
parents don't know Emily," he said. "If they did they
would understand why you got in trouble yesterday."

I nodded. Malik had his own troubles with Emily.
Since the first day of school, she had tried to beat his
score on every math test and every social studies report. Last week she had gotten a better grade on the
science test. Malik refused to talk about it, that's how
upset he was.

"Emily Scott acts like she owns the world," I muttered. "If we're not good enough for her, then why
won't she leave us alone?"

"You embarrassed her," Malik pointed out. "She
thought everyone was laughing at her. Nobody likes
to be embarrassed."

"Falling down is nothing," I muttered. "She
doesn't even know the meaning of embarrassment.
After all, she shoved me into the girls' bathroom."
I didn't add that I knew something even worse—
a grandfather who forgot things like getting dressed
and wearing teeth.

"But she thinks you tripped her on purpose," Malik
pointed out. We had reached the front of our school.
A bunch of kids were hanging around the front door.

Of course, Emily was right there on the top step, staring down like a vulture eyeing its next meal.

"Hey, Malik," she said. "I'll make you a deal. Tell me what's in that pack and I'll let you through the door."

"Ignore her," I whispered as we climbed the steps. "It's the best way to deal with bullies."

But Emily was not the kind of kid who is easily ignored.

"I have decided to solve the Dooley Elementary backpack mystery," Emily said. "Everyone is dying to know, so I'm going to tell them. There is absolutely nothing you can do to stop me."

Emily stepped in front of me and poked my chest to make her point crystal clear. Unfortunately, when she did, I tripped over the toe of her ultra-white sneaker. It wouldn't have been so bad but my foot slipped off the step's edge and I lost my balance. I dropped my books and reached out, grabbing for something to stop me from falling. Anything.

My fingers found Malik's backpack. "Let go!" Malik yelled, but it was too late.

The backpack roller-coastered off Malik's arm and thudded to the steps, the strap still wrapped around my fingers. I slid down, step by step, dragging the backpack with me until I landed on the ground. I'm pretty sure I heard something break inside Malik's backpack.

"What did you do?" Malik yelled. He galloped back down the steps and kneeled next to his backpack as if I had just killed it.

I reached for Malik's pack. "I'll fix it for you," I said.

Malik jerked the strap out of my grasp and cradled the pack in his arms like it was a dying puppy. From inside came a rattling sound.

"It wasn't my fault," I told him. "Blame Emily."

Malik was blinking again, but this time it wasn't because he was trying to think. It was because there were tears in his eyes. "You're the one that did it. I told you to let go!"

And then my best friend turned away from me, marched up the steps, pushed past Emily, and disappeared inside Dooley Elementary.

"I'm going to make you pay for that," I told Emily. I had one foot on the steps, ready to let her have it.

"Yeah?" Emily asked. "You and what army?"

The girls standing behind Emily giggled. I glared at them. Sharissa and Barbara had been in my class for the last two years. How could they side with Emily—a complete stranger?

"You better hurry," Sharissa said in a singsongy voice.

"Or your homework will end up in Timbuktu," Barbara added.

"And Mr. Simon will be mad," Emily added.

My spelling homework had blown halfway back to the playground, and books were scattered on the ground around my sneaker. My agenda fluttered open to the page where Dad had drawn a smiley face. I growled at it as I bent over to pick up my books.

By the time I had chased down my homework, the principal was standing at the top of the steps, her hands on her hips. "The bell is getting ready to ring," Mrs. Hollis said with a frown. "Hurry. You're going to be late."

"It wasn't my fault," I tried to tell her, but she stopped me with a quick shake of her head.

"I don't have time to listen to your excuses, Logan. Get to class."

I hugged my books to my chest and started running.

"WALK!" Mrs. Hollis yelled after me.

"But you said hurry!" I blurted. It was, after all, the truth.

Hollis the Hawk crossed her arms over her chest

and peered down at me over her glasses. "Watch the sass," she warned.

"Great," I muttered to the cracks in the cement blocks of the wall. "The day hasn't even started and I've already made my best friend mad and gotten into trouble with the principal. And it's all thanks to Emily, the Snot, Scott."

9

Poop Head

I skidded around the corner to my classroom and almost ran right into Emily standing in front of the water fountain. A bunch of other kids circled her like wasps swarming a nest.

I couldn't figure out why Sharissa and Barbara laughed as if Emily were the funniest thing since the invention of wedgies. "I bet Logan knows," Emily said loud enough to echo down the hall.

"What?" I muttered, trying to push past Sharissa and Barbara.

"He has to know," Sharissa said.

"He's probably known forever," Barbara added.

"Know what?" I asked again.

"What Malik has in his pack," Emily said. "It must be something really important, because he carries it wherever he goes."

"Is it a dangerous chemical that he's not supposed to have?" Barbara asked.

This wasn't such a weird guess, since everyone knew Malik did science experiments for fun on the weekends.

"It's *his* backpack," I said through gritted teeth. "He has the right to keep whatever's inside to himself if he wants to."

"You *do* know what's inside, don't you? You're just not telling," Emily said. Her grin was the kind of smile you'd expect to see on a vampire just before swooping in to suck your blood.

I wasn't about to admit that I'd been trying to find out, too. I pushed past Emily and the other girls, but Emily blocked my way. "If it's something dangerous, I should warn Mr. Simon," she said.

"Leave Malik alone," I told her.

"It *is* dangerous," she said. "I can tell by the way you're avoiding my question. Everyone knows that a guilty person avoids answering."

"I told you, nobody knows what's inside. Now drop it," I said.

A few more kids crowded closer.

"We don't believe you, Logan," Emily said. "We all think you know what's inside. Maybe it's something horrible. Like pickled eyeballs or dog poop!"

By the way Sharissa laughed, she must have thought that was the funniest thing she'd ever heard. Emily stood tall in the middle of the group, looking like she was the star of a sitcom. I couldn't believe the other kids in my class were falling for it hook, line, and sinker. I had to do something before it got out of hand.

"How did you guess?" I asked.

Emily stopped smiling. I had her confused. "What?" she asked.

Now the rest of the kids were quiet, too. Emily's eyes briefly reminded me of the way Grandpa looked when he forgot where he had put his dentures.

"Yep," I said. I leaned forward like I was telling a secret. "That's what it is, all right, but it isn't just *any* dog poop. It's special."

"Oh, no," Barbara said, suddenly realizing I was doing what I did best.

"Tall Tale Logan strikes again," Sharissa said, her

eyes rolling so far back in her head I bet she could see her ponytail.

Randy and Bobby nodded. "Tell us, Logan. What kind is it?"

They were laughing again, but now they were laughing with me instead of with Emily.

"It's like you said. Malik has been doing experiments. Science experiments. He's developing a special dog food," I explained in a low voice.

Even though most of the kids knew I was just telling another story, they all leaned forward so they wouldn't miss a word. Nobody was looking at Emily anymore. They were looking at me. It was time for a real zinger.

I looked right at Emily and said, "It's hard work, but very important. If he succeeds, he's sure to make millions from his invention, because Malik is working on a food that won't make dog poop smell like *you*!"

The crowd of kids clustered around us laughed so loud Mr. Simon came to the door. "Everyone inside," he said. "Now!" He was looking at me like I had done something wrong.

I couldn't help but notice that Emily's face was red when she marched past me and slammed her books on her desk. My day might have started out bad, but knowing I had gotten the best of Emily had made everything worthwhile.

Mr. Simon started each day with writing workshop. He believed that good writing came from good ideas. He never told us what to write, only what kind of writing to do. We were supposed to write a piece that persuaded someone to do something. He said it was up to us to think of a topic that was important. The stupid picture Dad had drawn in my agenda gave me my idea.

THE PERFECT PET, I wrote in big block letters at the top of my journal. Underneath I started a list. Next to number one I listed SNAKE.

A snake, after all, would be a very unusual pet. I didn't know anybody else who had one. Plus, it would be fun to scare girls with. I couldn't help but grin at the thought of Emily Scott running clear to the next county to get away from a hissing snake. Of course, Mom hadn't seemed too happy about the idea when I had mentioned it. And it's not like I could do much with a pet snake. It couldn't play fetch. I couldn't take it for a walk. Couldn't teach it tricks. That gave me another idea.

Under SNAKE I wrote DOG. Everybody knew a dog made a good pet. Not much to think about. A

dog would be an okay pet, but lots of kids had dogs—
nothing original there.

I stared out the window and chewed the tip of my
pencil, trying to think of the pet I would get at the
end of two weeks. The possibilities were endless.
Mouse, lizard, tarantula. I imagined all the things I
could do with each one.

Mr. Simon interrupted my thinking. "Logan?
Have you started your writing assignment yet?" His
eyebrows were arched so high I thought they might
crack his forehead.

I bent over my paper and added the ideas to my
list. I had gotten my list all the way up to fifteen when
the egg timer on Mr. Simon's desk went off, telling us
writing time was over. Mr. Simon set the timer for everything. It had gotten so I really hated hearing that
ding.

Emily's arm flew up in the air. "I want to share,
Mr. Simon," she said.

Mr. Simon nodded, and Emily pranced to the front
of the room as if she were leading a parade. "'Don't
Be a Ratfink or You'll Lose All Your Friends,'" Emily read in a loud, clear voice. "By Emily Scott," she
added, as if we didn't already know who she was.

Emily paused when there was a knock on the door.

"Go ahead, Emily," Mr. Simon said, and then he ducked out into the hallway to talk to the fifth-grade teacher from next door.

As soon as Mr. Simon left the room, Emily started to read like her journal was the Declaration of Independence.

"Kids should not be ratfinks. A ratfink is an obnoxious, and if you ask me, totally untrustworthy person. A perfect example of a ratfink is someone, and I won't mention any names, who would tell his best friend's secret just so he could be popular. In other words, a ratfink is a despicable person who rats on his friends."

I couldn't believe it. Everyone knew exactly who she was writing about even if she didn't use any names. Me. In her journal piece she said I bragged about how I knew what was in Malik's backpack. "He told everyone that his best friend collected poop from the biggest dogs."

"Hey!" I blurted. "That's not true."

"Is too," Emily snapped. "Everyone knows you think Malik's backpack is a menace to our classroom. We heard you say it this morning. Then you told everybody that he keeps dog poop in there. I'm not the only one who heard it."

Sharissa and Barbara were nodding. So were some other kids.

Everything had gone horribly wrong. Without Mr. Simon to call a halt to it, the rest of the class was siding with Emily. Everyone but Malik. He sat in his chair, trying to stuff his backpack under his desk so no one would notice it.

I jumped out of my seat just as Mr. Simon came back in the room.

"You're nothing but a big fat liar!" I yelled.

"Mr. Malone," Mr. Simon said. His voice came from deep in his chest and sounded as hard as steel. "Sit down. Now. Or else."

He didn't have to finish the sentence. Be quiet or else I would get a stupid frown face drawn in my agenda. I plopped back in my seat and looked at Malik. Giant splotches covered his cheeks. He slid down in his chair until his chin nearly rested on the top of his desk.

"Don't believe her," I hissed.

Malik didn't hear. How could he? The rest of the class was laughing so loud I doubt he could have heard an elephant stampede.

I tried telling Malik the truth at lunch, but he didn't save a place for me. Instead, I sat at the end of the table and ate my bologna sandwich alone. Emily, on the other hand, sat in the middle of a group of girls. The kids around her listened as though she were a queen. Every once in a while they looked over at me and giggled.

Recess wasn't much better. Malik sat by the fence, his back resting against the chain link. "I have to talk to you," I said.

Malik didn't look at me. He stared straight ahead. "Everyone's calling me Poop Head," he said. "Thanks to you."

"It didn't happen the way Emily said it did," I told him.

Malik didn't let me explain. He got right to the point. "Did you or did you not tell everyone I kept poop in my backpack?" Malik asked.

"Not really," I said.

Blink, blink. Blink. "Not really?" he asked. "What kind of answer is that? Either you said it or you didn't. Which is it?"

"I did say it, but—"

Malik didn't let me finish. "And I thought you were my friend," he said. "Emily is right. You *are* a ratfink, and you are definitely the worst best friend in the entire fifth grade."

Malik pushed himself up from the ground and walked away, leaving me sitting alone by the fence.

Word got around fast on the playground. By the end of recess, I was officially known as Ratfink to just about everybody.

"No cuts, 'Fink," Sharissa said when I lined up to go inside. Randy and Barbara heard her and giggled.

"Out of the way, 'Fink," Bobby said when he shoved me away from the water fountain.

"Who're you going to rat on next?" Allison asked when we went to the computer lab.

Emily laughed so hard she snorted.

I was the only kid in school who knew who the real ratfink was. Emily. But there wasn't a thing I could do about it.

That's exactly what was going through my head when Emily raised her hand right before the bell rang to end the worst day of my life.

"I'll empty the pencil sharpener," she offered in a sickeningly sweet voice.

Mr. Simon smiled at her like she was the star of a Broadway show. "Thank you, Emily."

She pranced down the aisle between our desks to get the barrel full of shavings. It happened so fast there wasn't time to think. I stuck out my foot right as she waltzed by on her way back. Emily teetered, trying to catch her balance. Shreds of wood and lead flew through the air.

And then Emily, the Snot, Scott fell flat on her behind.

10

World's Greatest Dad

The next morning Dad stared down at my agenda lying open on the table. The circle with a frown that Mr. Simon had drawn at the bottom of Friday's column was easy to see even from where I stood by the refrigerator. Mr. Simon had pressed so hard with his red pen that it had torn the paper. A curl of steam from Dad's WORLD'S GREATEST DAD coffee mug circled his hand, making it look like his fingers were burning.

Since Grandpa had moved in, Saturdays meant Dad sat at the table and paid bills while Mom and Grandpa went to the grocery store. This morning, Dad had shoved the pile of bills and the checkbook to the side of the kitchen table. The only sound in the house was the hum of the refrigerator.

"Have a seat, Logan," Dad said after I'd filled a bowl with cereal and milk.

I sat. The cereal in my bowl was getting soggy, but I figured I better not move until Dad said something.

Finally, he spoke. "You couldn't make it one day?" His voice was quiet. Too quiet. "Not one single day?"

"It was Emily's fault. She—"

Dad's hand flew up to stop my words in midair, nearly knocking over his coffee mug on the way. "You made a deal, Logan. You were going to behave for two weeks straight. That's only ten school days. It had nothing to do with anybody named Emily."

"But she—"

"I don't want to hear another word about Emily," Dad warned me. He took a deep breath, and I knew he was trying to stay calm.

"But—"

"No more excuses," Dad said before I could finish my sentence. "And no more lies." This time his voice had risen from fake-calm to almost-mad. He took another deep breath, so his next words came out low and slow. "Your mother and I agree with Mr. Simon. This storytelling of yours has gotten way out of hand."

"You don't say anything when Grandpa lies about why he can't remember my name or where he put his teeth."

"This isn't about your grandfather," Dad said. "It's about you. You have to accept responsibility for your own actions. I'm saying this for your own good, Logan. Nobody likes a liar."

"How do you know I'm the one lying?" I blurted. "You haven't even given me a chance to tell my side of the story."

"Enough, Logan."

"It's not enough!" My own voice was getting louder and louder, just like his. I jumped up, pushing the chair back so hard it left a black mark across the linoleum. "You believe everything Mr. Simon writes in that notebook, but he doesn't know the whole story."

"Sit down," Dad ordered, "and watch your tone of voice."

I didn't sit down. I didn't stop yelling, either. "I have to yell just to get you to hear me!"

Dad's voice rose a couple more notches. "When you were in first grade, even second grade, your stories were cute. But you're in fifth grade, Logan. You keep saying you want to be in middle school. Well, a middle school kid doesn't tell stories. Your lies are downright embarrassing."

"Embarrassing?" I shouted, and I had to admit that I didn't sound very respectful even to my own ears.

"Watch it, Logan," Dad warned. His cheeks were bright red now, and he had forgotten all about taking deep breaths.

His warning came too late. Words were building inside me like bubbles in a shaken can of soda, and there was nothing I could do to keep them from bursting out. "What do *you* know about embarrassing?" I asked. "Every day you put on your tie and jacket and drive to a nice quiet office where you add up neat lines of numbers and forget that I have to worry whether or not Grandpa is wandering around the neighborhood in a pink tutu. What if the kids find out about him? What if Grandpa shows up outside school wearing a snorkel and a rubber ducky raft? I'd never be able to live it down if Emily Scott found out the truth about Grandpa. Never in a million years!"

"You're exaggerating," Dad said.

"That's easy for you to say," I told him. "You don't have to put up with Emily, whose one mission in life is to make me look like a fool. If she found out about Grandpa she would *never* let me live it down."

The color in Dad's face seemed to slip right off his cheeks and into his coffee mug when his hand slapped the table. Hard. Coffee splashed out of his mug and splattered his newspaper. "For the last time, this has nothing to do with your grandfather or with some girl in your class. This is about YOU. Accept responsibility for your own behavior and stop blaming everyone else. Not me. Not your mother or grandfather. And definitely not some girl named Emily."

I was about to tell him he was wrong, wrong, and more wrong, but just then the kitchen door flew open. Grandpa held a bag of groceries in one arm and he saluted us with the other. "Never fear! The food regiment is here," he announced as if he were getting ready to march into battle.

Mom pushed Grandpa aside and gave my dad a look that could have soured the milk in my cereal bowl. "We have got to talk," Mom hissed. She rolled her eyes back at Grandpa. "This is *not* working."

"Can't this wait, Joyce?" Dad asked.

The look Mom gave Dad was all the answer he needed. I knew that look. It was nice knowing that, for once, Dad was on the other end of Mom's don't-you-mess-with-me-if-you-know-what's-good-for-you look.

"Help your grandfather with the groceries, Logan," Dad said.

And just like that our conversation was over. End of discussion. The World's Greatest Dad had spoken.

I grabbed my jacket, pushed past Grandpa, and stomped out the door. Dad didn't try to stop me.

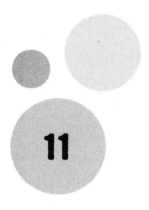

11

Tooth and Claw

Without thinking, I headed for Malik's house. He lived two blocks down and one street over. I stopped in front of his house. He wasn't on the porch. No use knocking on his door, because Malik was still mad at me.

I had absolutely nothing to do and nowhere to go, and it was all Emily Scott's fault.

I stomped past Malik's house and headed for the neighborhood park three blocks away. A couple kids were on the seesaws. Nobody my age was around. I plopped on a swing. Every time I passed close to the ground I kicked up a cloud of dirt, until my sneakers and jeans had turned a dull brown.

"Mind if I join you, Charlie?"

"Logan," I muttered as I twisted the chains to look over my shoulder. Grandpa stood there, a bag of Oreos in each hand.

"Where'd you get those?" I asked. Mom didn't usually buy more than one pack of cookies at a time. I couldn't believe Grandpa got by with two.

Grandpa looked down at the cookies in his hands as if he were seeing them for the first time. "They're your favorite kind," Grandpa said instead of answering my question. "I remembered that."

I didn't have the heart to tell him that Oreos were my favorite cookies when I was five. Now I preferred peanut butter.

Grandpa plopped in the swing next to me and held out a bag.

"Cookies won't help," I said, but I took one anyway.

Grandpa grinned. I was glad to see he hadn't lost his teeth again, but now there were cookie crumbs stuck between them. He held out the package again and I took another. "Chocolate can cure a lot of things," he said matter-of-factly.

"There is no cure for my problem," I mumbled.

"So tell me," Grandpa said after eating another cookie. "What exactly is your problem?"

I looked at my grandfather. He looked totally happy with his arms looped around the chains and a package of cookies in each hand. Finally, an adult was willing to listen to my side of the story, but it was just my luck that it was the one person who wouldn't remember a thing about it. I told him about Emily anyway.

"Ah," Grandpa said. "A girl problem. My specialty." Grandpa wiggled his eyebrows and gave me a wink.

I couldn't imagine Grandpa knowing anything about girls. Especially girls like Emily.

"Sounds like this young lady is trying to get your attention," Grandpa said.

"She's getting attention, all right," I said, biting into another cookie. Mom would be mad when she found out I had eaten enough cookies to ruin a month of dinners, but I didn't care. "Emily loves making everyone laugh at me. It's what she lives for."

The chains on the swings creaked as Grandpa and

I moved back and forth. He was quiet and I figured he had forgotten the entire conversation, but he surprised me when he spoke again. "There are worse things than being laughed at, Charlie," Grandpa said.

"Logan," I said without thinking. "And you're wrong. Believe me, there is nothing worse than being the butt of everyone's joke."

Grandpa nodded. "It's hard walking into a new place. Being the one person that stands out in a crowd, the one that doesn't fit in with the rest. It's like waking up from sleepwalking to find yourself in a foreign land where everyone is staring at you. You feel like you have to do something quick to make them stop staring," Grandpa said. "Like make them laugh so they won't notice the real you."

I got the feeling that Grandpa wasn't talking about Emily anymore. I dragged my foot to make my swing stop.

"You have to find the right words," Grandpa continued. "Know what to do and say. You know what it feels like? It feels like being a chicken with its head cut off."

I realized Grandpa was new just like Emily—new to our house, new to our family's way of doing things. New to the neighborhood and city. I was just starting to feel sorry for him when Grandpa suddenly pushed out of the swing, tucked his hands under his armpits, and began strutting around the swing set like a giant chicken. He lifted his chin to the sky. "Cock-a-doodle-doo!" he yodeled.

I jumped off the swing and grabbed Grandpa. Any sympathy I might have had for him disappeared faster than a popping balloon. I looked around to make sure nobody I knew had seen my grandfather doing a chicken dance in the middle of the park. "Stop that," I hissed. "You can't go around acting like a chicken. People will laugh."

"Now you're getting it," Grandpa said. "Making people laugh keeps them from seeing what you don't want them to see. That's what this Emily is doing. She's just walked into a scary forest, and she's afraid none of the birds there will like the color of her feathers, so she's acting totally outrageous to keep anyone from noticing."

Nothing Grandpa was saying made any sense. "It's a school, not a forest," I said. I talked slowly, hoping it would sink into Grandpa's muddled brain. "There are no birds there. Emily Scott doesn't have a single feather."

Grandpa laughed. Loud. Then he gave me a hug.

Not just a little one, either. This hug was so big I felt the cookies that got caught between us being crushed into crumbs. "Don't worry about your girlfriend," Grandpa said.

"She is *not* my girlfriend," I said through clenched teeth, and pushed him away. "And I can't wait to get to school on Monday, because I'm going to let Emily have it. She's gotten me in trouble one time too many."

"Fighting with your girlfriend will just land you in a big mess again," Grandpa pointed out.

I sighed. "I told you, she is *not* my girlfriend. Weren't you listening? At this rate, I'll never earn two weeks' worth of stupid smiley faces. I might as well kiss the pet idea goodbye."

"Pet?" Grandpa asked as he sat back on the swing. The squeaking chains sounded like teeth chewing on aluminum foil.

I told Grandpa the deal Mom and Dad had made. "I was supposed to get a pet when I turned ten," I told him. I knew it sounded mean, but I couldn't stop myself from adding, "But Mom and Dad changed their mind when you came."

Grandpa didn't say anything for a few swings. "I guess I sort of messed things up for you. First I took over the basement and now this. I'm sorry. But things might change for the better if your mother gets her way."

Grandpa sounded so normal. And serious. That's how he was. One minute he was acting like a chicken and the next he was perfectly normal. "What does Mom want?" I asked.

Grandpa completely ignored my question. "Maybe I can make up for all this by helping you."

"How can you help me?"

"With a little friendly advice," Grandpa explained. "If you concentrate on getting a pet instead of thinking about getting even, you might be able to ignore Emily long enough to get Mr. Simon off your case."

"Impossible."

"Maybe not," he said. "You still want a pet, don't you?"

"Of course I do."

"Then let me help you focus," Grandpa said. "What kind of pet do you want?"

I sat on the swing next to Grandpa so I could think. A girl with a dog walked by on the sidewalk. "A dog would make an awesome pet," I said. "I'd get a big one. Huge. His name would be Brutus, and I'd teach him to growl and drip slobber whenever Emily the Snot pranced by."

When the girl walking her dog wouldn't throw a stick, her dog started barking. It wasn't a little bark, either. It was the kind that echoed all over the park and made people look.

"What if your giant dog barked when you were at school?" Grandpa asked. "If I know your mother, she wouldn't be too happy about that. She likes things quiet. Quiet, orderly, and normal."

He didn't have to say it for us both to realize that my mother thought Grandpa was exactly the opposite of those things.

"Think smaller," Grandpa suggested. "And a lot quieter. How about if we go to the pet store and have a look around? You just might find the pet worth working for."

I jumped off the swing. "Now you're talking," I said. "I need to find out about my choices. Follow me."

I was so excited that Grandpa practically had to run to keep up with me. I didn't stop until we reached the Tooth and Claw Pet Emporium.

A gust of cold air-conditioning slapped my face when Grandpa and I entered the pet store. Bells hanging above the door clanged, and the clerk looked up.

The Tooth and Claw wasn't like one of those big warehouse stores. It was a small neighborhood shop nestled between Louis's Snip-It Barbershop and Delma's Oh-Sew-Fine Store. The Tooth and Claw was big enough for three rows of shelves down the middle. Puppies romped around in the front window. Fish and birds were toward the back against the left wall. The back of the store was lined with cages filled with hamsters, gerbils, mice, lizards, and snakes.

I breathed in the smell of cedar chips and disinfectant. I'd been here before—lots of times. The clerk behind the counter recognized me and didn't bother asking if we needed any help. I was heading down the left aisle toward the back when I realized Grandpa wasn't behind me anymore.

Squeak. Squeak. Squeak-squeak-squeak!

I hurried back the way I had come. Grandpa was standing in front of some dog toys, squeezing everything he could get his hands on. "Stop it," I hissed and grabbed his elbow.

"Did you notice the pitch is slightly higher in the red ball than in the purple bone?" he asked as if he were conducting a scientific study.

"Who cares," I said.

Grandpa stopped to look at a fish the size of my fist. "Fish," he said. "They're the ultimate in quiet."

I peered through the water. "Maybe I could get one with pointy teeth that eats raw meat," I thought out loud. Then I shook my head. "I doubt I could get Emily to stick her hand in the tank, though."

"Did you know watching fish swim lowers blood pressure?" Grandpa asked.

I looked at Grandpa like he'd sprouted fins and scales. "How do you know that kind of stuff?"

Grandpa tapped his forehead with his finger. "It's all up here, Charlie."

"Logan," I muttered, and turned my back on Grandpa. He didn't hear me. He'd gotten distracted by a shelf with aquarium supplies. He bent over and picked up a colorful castle.

I was not interested in fish castles.

Birds were perched in cages next to the fish. "Polly want a cracker?" I asked a green bird with yellow tail feathers.

"Birds. They live to be quite old," Grandpa said, looking over my shoulder. "A big responsibility, taking care of something in its old age."

"Maybe I could teach it to say cuss words whenever Emily got near me," I said. "That would be fun."

I heard the bells over the front door ring as someone entered.

Grandpa had already moved down the aisle and was standing in front of a row of cages at the back of the store. For an old man, he could move fast. I hurried to catch up with him.

"How about a rabbit?" Grandpa asked. "Did you know that a female rabbit is called a doe and starts breeding at the age of six months? It only takes her thirty days to have a litter. Then she's ready to breed again. Let's see, that means in a year's time . . ."

I grabbed Grandpa's elbow again. "This is no time for a math lesson," I told him as something else caught my eye. "Perfect," I said, peering into a cage down by the floor.

Grandpa bent down to look over my shoulder. "A rat?"

"Look at that one in the back. The one with beady eyes. It reminds me a little bit of Emily," I said. "I could take it to school and shove it in her face. I can almost hear her screaming now! That rat would be perfect. I wish I could pet him."

Grandpa grinned. "Would that make you happy, Charlie? Would it? Well, I can take care of that," he said, and reached for the cage door.

I pointed to a sign on the wall that said to ask for assistance. "We're not supposed to open the cages," I said.

"Rules, rules, rules," Grandpa nearly sang. "You sound like your mother. Don't do this. Don't do that.

We're just going to say howdy-doody to the one you have your eye on."

He flicked open the latch and reached toward the rat in the back. Grandpa moved slowly, careful not to startle him. His fingers had just reached the rat's head when something happened. Something terrible.

"BOO!"

Emily Scott jumped out from behind a stand of chew toys.

"AHHHH!" I screamed. Unfortunately, when I jumped back I bumped Grandpa. Grandpa landed on the floor. I fell right over him and landed with my back against the giant aquarium that was at the end of an aisle. The stand wobbled. It swayed. Then it crashed to the floor.

That's when the rats scrambled out of the cage and scurried across Grandpa's shoe.

"AHHHH!" I yelled again when the rats splashed through the water on the floor.

"AHHHH!" the clerk screamed when he saw the herd of rats heading his way.

Of course, there was one person in the Tooth and Claw Pet Emporium who wasn't screaming. Emily Scott.

She was too busy laughing.

12

Squawk!

"Stop those rats!" the salesclerk yelled.

One rat went left. Two ran right. Another one darted between the clerk's legs. But Emily, the biggest rat of them all, hightailed it out the front door, leaving me and Grandpa to face the wrath of, by now, a very red-faced clerk.

"You are in *so* much trouble," the clerk said.

There was no point arguing. I lunged for a tail as it slipped between two displays. I had to move fast.

Really fast. That's why I didn't see the shelf full of dog bowls. They smashed to the floor with a sound that brought all of us to a dead halt. Even the rats.

"What have you done?" the clerk yelled. I didn't bother answering. After all, it was obvious.

The rat sidestepped the broken bowls and back-tracked toward Grandpa.

"Catch him," I yelled, my sneakers slipping on the broken ceramic.

Grandpa looked at me as if I were speaking Swahili.

"The rat!" I repeated. "Get it."

The rat's whiskers quivered as he passed Grandpa's shoes. Grandpa absentmindedly scooted his foot out of the way.

A big bird with white feathers sticking straight up from its head squawked, and Grandpa turned away from me to face the bird. "Why, I do believe you're talking to me," Grandpa said. Then he tucked his hands under his armpits and, for the second time that day, became a bird. "Squawk," he said back to the bird. "Squawk! Squawk! SQUAWK!"

The clerk's mouth dropped open, and he stared as Grandpa squawked all the way down the aisle. I could tell he didn't know what to do about an old man pretending to be a bird. I knew exactly how the clerk felt. I didn't know what to do, either. I could feel the tips of my ears burning. If ever the earth was going to open up and swallow somebody, I thought this would be the perfect time.

The bells over the door jangled when Grandpa pulled it open. The clerk and I watched as Grandpa "flew" out of the store and squawked down the street.

I looked around. Nobody else was in the store. The only one who had seen my grandfather acting like a dodo bird was the clerk. At least Emily was long gone. If she had seen the whole thing I'm sure she would have raced back home and sent an e-mail to everyone in the school telling them what had happened.

I helped catch all the rats. Then I mopped up the aquarium water and swept up the broken dog bowls. I thought that was pretty generous considering none of this was my fault in the first place.

"I'm sorry," I told the clerk as I dumped the last of the broken dishes into a garbage can. They landed with a loud clunk in the bottom.

"Not as sorry as you're going to be," he snapped.

I looked at the clerk. "What do you mean?"

"Somebody's got to pay for the broken stuff," he said. "And that somebody is YOU!" He jabbed a finger right into my chest. "I already called the owner. You better call your parents, because you are in trouble. B-I-G trouble."

My dad and the owner showed up at the same time. The owner's name was Mrs. Harrison. She shook Dad's hand and then looked at the clerk.

"Tell us what happened, Mitchell," she said.

"This kid let all the rats out," the clerk said.

"Wait," I interrupted. "That's not true. Grandpa—"

Dad's hand smacked the counter, stopping my words in midair. "Logan," Dad said, "your grandfather isn't even here. Now, let Mitchell finish."

Mitchell narrowed his eyes at me. "Like I said. He opened the cage even though there's a sign that says not to. Then he knocked over the aquarium and all those designer bowls. The ones people can personalize with Rover's name."

"I didn't do it on purpose," I blurted. "I was trying to help catch the rats."

"I know, Logan," Dad said. "You'd never do something like that on purpose. But you still are responsible."

"But he's telling it wrong," I argued. "None of this would have happened if it wasn't for Emily Scott—"

"Oh, for crying out loud," my dad yelped. "Not her again." Then he stopped and took a big breath. "I'm sorry my son caused a problem," he said, turning to face Mrs. Harrison. "He's really a good kid. Just a bit impulsive. We're working on getting him to accept responsibility for his actions."

"I have three boys of my own," Mrs. Harrison said as if I weren't even there. "The rats have been captured, so there's no loss there, but there's still the issue of the broken merchandise."

When Mrs. Harrison totaled the cost of the damages, I had to sit down on the stool behind the counter. Who would have thought that a big bowl of water could cost so much? Even if I saved my allowance for a year I wouldn't have enough. I decided then and there that an aquarium was not what I wanted.

"I have an idea," Dad said. And then he told us his plan.

"No way," I said when he was finished. "I'm not coming here every day after school to clean up after animals."

"Yes, you will," Dad said. "As long as Mrs. Harrison agrees to let you work to pay off the cost of the broken bowls. Consider it an amendment to Mr. Simon's deal. You not only have to behave at school, but you also have to accept responsibility outside of school."

"But—"

Dad held up that hand again. He wasn't going to let me say a word. He looked at the store owner. "What do you say?" he asked. "This is entirely up to you."

Mrs. Harrison thought long and hard. She looked at me as if she were trying to memorize every freckle on my nose. "Make sure you're on time," she finally said, "and you've got yourself a job."

13

Wrong, Wrong, WRONG!

"Just wait until I tell Mom," I told Dad when he pulled into our driveway. "I'm pretty sure Oprah and Dr. Phil would say that forcing a little kid like me to work is wrong, wrong, WRONG!"

Dad gripped the steering wheel with white knuckles. "I'm not forcing you to work," he said in a fake-calm voice. "This is a decision you made when you let those rats out. You have to accept responsibility for your actions, Logan."

"But it wasn't me," I argued. "I didn't do it."

"Logan," Dad said as he put the car in park. "The clerk saw the entire thing."

I slammed the door on Dad's words. I didn't wait for him to get out of the car. I raced up the three steps to our house and pushed open the back door.

Mom stood at the counter, chopping carrots and tossing them in a stew pot.

"You're not going to believe what Dad is making me do," I said before she even had a chance to turn around. "You have to stop him."

Mom went on chopping carrots as if the world wasn't about to end.

"Did you hear me?" I asked.

Mom glanced my way. "I hear you loud and clear," she said. "In fact, I wouldn't be surprised if they could hear you on the space station."

"This is no time for jokes," I said. "Dad has seriously lost it this time. He's nuttier than Grandpa!"

"That's not funny," Mom said. Her voice was as hard as the chopping board. "Don't talk about your grandfather like that. Just because he's having some trouble remembering things, it doesn't mean he's crazy."

"But Dad is out of control. You have to stop him."

"From what I heard," Mom said, "it was *you* that was out of control. Not your father. After all, he didn't wreak havoc in a pet store."

It felt like a basketball had slammed into my stomach. "How . . . how did you know?" I asked when I found my voice again.

Mom tossed a handful of carrots in the pot. "Cell phone," she said. "I know everything, Logan. Everything."

"You don't actually *agree* with Dad, do you?" I asked, letting a little hope slip into my voice.

"One hundred percent," she said.

The basketball whomped into my stomach again.

"We love you, Logan," Mom continued, "but we can't bail you out every time you make a mistake. Working to pay for what you broke is the right thing to do."

"You bail out Grandpa," I huffed. "You and Dad make excuses for him all the time."

The knife in Mom's hand froze three inches above another doomed carrot. It hovered there while Mom took a deep breath. "I told you, Logan," she finally said. "Do not bring your grandfather into this." Then her knife whacked the carrot in half.

When Dad came in it was as if nothing in the world

was wrong. He helped cut up celery and potatoes, and my parents laughed about something they had read in the newspaper.

I stomped up to my room and tried concentrating on the novel Mr. Simon had assigned. I was reading the same paragraph for the fifth time when I heard Mom yell up the stairs.

"Dinner!"

I slammed the book closed. I didn't want to face my parents, but my stomach was growling and the roast smelled really good. I headed down the steps for the kitchen.

"Where's your grandfather, Logan?" Dad asked when I appeared.

"How should I know?" I asked back. "I'm not his babysitter."

"Of course you're not," Dad said. "We just thought you might know where he is, since he likes spending time with you."

"He must've fallen asleep in his room," Mom said. "I haven't seen him all afternoon. Go tell him dinner is ready, Logan."

My parents had told me, in no uncertain terms, that the basement was now Grandpa's domain. I was only allowed to go there when he invited me. Or like now, when I had to fetch him like a pair of bedroom slippers.

The door at the top of the steps was standing slightly open. The bottom step disappeared in shadows. "Grandpa?" I yelled down the stairs.

Silence.

I held the railing and went halfway down. "Grandpa?" I called into the shadows.

More silence.

When I got to the bottom of the steps I flipped on the switch. The first thing I saw was a sticky note on the wall that said, *My name is Charles Theodore Malone.*

I was so glad my parents hadn't named me exactly after my grandfather. Going around as Theodore instead of Logan would have been worse than being called Charlie.

I walked into the big room where I used to have my Pop-A-Shot game and Ping-Pong table. Now it was filled with a couch, recliner, and television. "Grandpa?" I called back toward his bedroom.

Grandpa didn't answer. I was about to head back upstairs when I noticed more sticky notes. They were everywhere. On the wall above the couch. Next to the television. Near his bedroom door. I walked around

the room, reading Grandpa's back-slanted handwriting.

I was born on November 30.

I married Meredith O'Conner on April 12.

My son's name is Paul.

Paul was born on July 15.

My daughter-in-law's name is Joyce.

Each note was a fact, a snippet of his life, something that I knew Grandpa was trying to remember. He had posted them in plain sight so he wouldn't forget to read them every day.

I pushed open the door to Grandpa's bedroom and flipped on the switch. Grandpa wasn't there. His room was empty, the bed still made. I turned, ready to head up the steps, when the pages of a notebook on his bedside table caught my attention.

Mr. Simon had always told us that what we wrote in journals was our own business. Private. That we should never snoop. But Grandpa's notebook was open. It wasn't really snooping. All I had to do was walk over toward his bed and I could see the familiar back-slanted script.

It looked like a grocery list, but this had nothing to do with food. My name was at the very top of the page. Below it was a list of facts.

My birthday.

My favorite color, sport, and television show.

The fact that I liked Oreo cookies.

He even had listed Malik as my best friend.

I swallowed. Hard. The sticky notes. The list. I knew what they meant. Grandpa was trying to remember things from long ago—and from now. He was trying to hang on.

Grandpa was doing everything he could to remember me.

14

Missing

"He isn't down there," I announced as I galloped back up the steps and into the kitchen.

Mom stopped spooning vegetables onto a platter and looked at Dad. "Have you seen him?" Mom asked.

Dad shook his head. "Not since you got back from the grocery store."

They both looked at me. "When was the last time you saw Grandpa?" Dad asked.

"Like I tried to tell you earlier, he was at the pet store," I said. "We went there from the park."

"The park?" Mom repeated with a blank look on her face.

I nodded. "He followed me. He brought a couple bags of Oreos to share."

"Cookies?" Mom asked. "Where in the world did he get cookies?"

"Didn't you buy them at the grocery store?" Dad asked.

Mom's lips were pressed in a straight line. "No. I didn't buy cookies."

"Anyway, after the park he followed me to the pet store. We were going to look at pets. That's when he—"

"Forget what happened at the pet store, Logan," Dad said. "I already know that part. He wasn't there by the time I got there. Where did he go?"

I glared at Dad. He still wasn't letting me tell what really happened. I sighed. "He became a bird and flew out the door."

"Logan!" Mom screeched, nearly sounding like a bird herself. "That's not the least bit funny!"

"This is definitely no time for one of your stories," Dad warned.

"I'm not making this up!" I said. "Grandpa started flapping his arms like a big bird and pretended to fly out the door. He squawked the entire way down the sidewalk. That's the last I saw of him."

"Didn't you go after him?" Dad asked.

"I told you. I'm not his babysitter!" I said.

Mom put a hand on my shoulder. "Logan's right," she said.

"I am?"

She looked at Dad and they both started firing off shotgun sentences. It was like watching a tennis game.

First Mom: I told you this wasn't working.

Then Dad: Just because he's late for dinner, it doesn't mean we can't make this work.

Mom again: This isn't about being late for a meal.

Dad, after a big breath: Let's talk about this later. Right now we have to find him.

Mom with a nod: Where could he be?

Then Dad: He can't go far on foot.

Mom, sounding panicky: But he's been gone for hours!

Dad, starting to pace: He could be anywhere.

Mom, her voice trembling: What if he's hurt?

Dad stopped pacing and held Mom by the shoulders. "I'll take my car. You go in yours. That way we can cover more ground."

"What about dinner?" I asked as Dad grabbed his car keys off the kitchen counter and they both headed for the back door.

Mom glanced at the forgotten platter. Steam no longer rolled off the roast. "Go ahead and eat." Then she started rattling off her usual list of instructions whenever they left me alone. "Keep the doors locked and don't go anywhere."

"I'll be fine," I said, trying to stand up so I'd look taller. "After all, middle school kids stay by themselves all the time."

"You're not in middle school, mister," Mom reminded me. "And stay off the phone in case Grandpa tries to call."

With that, my parents left to search for Grandpa.

I helped myself to a plate of cold roast and then went back up to my room to try reading again. The words on the page blurred. All I could think about were the sticky notes filled with Grandpa's handwriting.

I knew Grandpa was having trouble remembering things, but I just thought it was like me forgetting what nine times seven was. But now I realized

Grandpa wasn't just forgetting names. He was forgetting his life. If he had trouble remembering my name, he could definitely have a problem remembering how to find his way back from the pet store, especially since he'd never been there before. The only reason he had gone was to help me feel better. In a way, I knew that made me a little bit responsible for the fact that Grandpa was missing.

I looked out the window and thought about what Mom had said. That this wasn't working. What did she mean by that?

The sun was hanging low in the sky. It would be night soon. I hated the idea of him wandering around in the dark.

Where could he be? I thought back to the last time I saw him. Hands tucked under his armpits, flapping his elbows. Squawking out the door. Pretending to be a bird. Just like he had in the park.

The park!

He knew how to get to the park. What if he went back there and was waiting? Waiting for me?

I slammed my book shut and headed out the door. Mom and Dad would never think about walking through the park, but I couldn't call them because I wasn't supposed to use the phone. I'd have to go look for him myself. I'd be home before Mom and Dad even knew I'd left, and then I'd be a hero for finding Grandpa.

I jogged the two blocks to the corner and turned on Foster Street. I slowed down as I passed Malik's house. He was on the porch, sitting on the top step, reading a book about chemistry. He was using his backpack as a backrest.

"Hey," I said.

He didn't answer. I knew he was still mad. If people called me Poop Head, I would be mad, too. I wanted to tell him I was sorry, but I had a feeling he wouldn't believe me. Nobody believed anything I said anymore.

"I'm looking for my grandfather," I said instead. "Have you seen him?"

Blink, blink. Blink.

I realized Malik couldn't figure out why I would be looking for a grown man. "He was with me this afternoon," I tried to explain. "But then he sort of disappeared. We think he might be lost."

"Lost?" Malik asked. "Why would your grandfather be lost? It's only three blocks to the park."

More than anything, I wanted to keep the truth about Grandpa a secret. I couldn't risk having the kids find out, because I knew what that would mean. Teasing for the rest of my days.

My brain went into hyperdrive, and story ideas started bouncing around in my brain like Ping-Pong balls. Maybe I could say Grandpa had been brainwashed by a gang of spies. Or that he had been hypnotized by a magician who forgot to snap his fingers. I could always tell Malik that aliens had abducted my real grandfather and transferred his memory into their spaceship communicator.

Of course, Malik would know they were stories, and his unanswered question would hang in the air between us. Not only that, Grandpa would still be wandering around somewhere. A story would just make everything worse. I had to tell Malik the truth.

"Promise not to tell?" I asked. "Anyone?"

"Tell what?" he asked. I knew he was more confused than ever by the way he was blinking.

Malik had been my best friend since the day we both grabbed the same purple crayon in kindergarten. If there was one person I could trust, it was him. I went up the steps and, without being invited, sat down next to Malik. "My grandpa has this problem," I said, trying to tell him without really saying it. "He sort of does weird things."

"Everybody's grandparents do weird things," Malik said. "My grandmother likes to sing Elvis Presley songs when she's taking bubble baths."

"This is different," I said. "Grandpa does really embarrassing things."

"Like what?" Malik said.

"Well, he forgets things. Like where he put his teeth. He never remembers my name is Logan. He also forgets to pay for things." Now that I was telling Malik, it was hard to stop.

"You mean your grandfather is a thief?" Malik asked.

"He doesn't mean to steal," I explained in a rush of air. "He just sees things and wants them, so he picks them up. He forgets that he's supposed to pay. Now we don't know where he is," I finished.

Malik's eyes narrowed. "You told me your grandfather was smart—smarter than the governor. You said he had a high-paying job and was a whiz at crunching numbers. Were those just more of your stories?"

"No, they were real," I said. "But all those things happened a long time ago. That's why he moved in with us. Dad said he needed help since he was starting to forget things. Nobody can know," I warned him. "It's really embarrassing the way he acts."

"It can't be that embarrassing," Malik said.

I nodded so hard I almost slipped off the step. "Believe me," I said. "It's bad." And then I told Malik what had happened at the pet store. "He pretended to be a bird and flew out of there, squawking all the way. Just think what would happen if Emily had seen that."

Malik sat long enough to listen to a mockingbird run through a couple of impersonations. Then he stood up and slipped the strap of his backpack over his left shoulder. "I'll help you look," he said.

And just like that, I knew Malik wasn't mad anymore. I was glad I'd told him the truth. It felt good having my best friend back.

15

Memory Snapshots

"You have to promise you won't tell a soul," I reminded Malik as we hurried to the park. "If Emily knew Grandpa danced like a chicken she'd call me Bird Brain until the day I died."

"Just like she calls me Poop Head," Malik said.

I grabbed Malik's elbow. "You know it didn't happen the way Emily said."

Malik pulled his elbow away. "I know, but I still hate being called Poop Head."

I couldn't blame Malik. Fifth graders are mean.

Once they latched onto a nickname, they wouldn't let it go the same way a tick hangs onto a dog. That was exactly why I couldn't let anyone at school find out about Grandpa.

It was getting dark fast, and the park had cleared out. The swings were empty.

No Grandpa.

"Maybe he's watching people play tennis," Malik said.

We headed for the courts where a bunch of teenagers were smacking tennis balls back and forth.

No Grandpa.

"How about the bleachers near the softball field?" Malik suggested.

We passed two teenagers cuddling on a bench. We were nearly to the field when Malik and I both spotted Grandpa.

He was sitting on the bleachers, alone. His shoulders were slumped and he looked much smaller than he really was. His eyes darted from the baseball field to the sidewalks to the empty pool. He had something in his hands that he kept turning over and over and over again.

"Grandpa?" I said when we got closer.

As soon as Grandpa saw me, his shoulders straightened and the two creases between his eyes disappeared. "Am I ever glad to see you, Charlie," Grandpa said. I could tell he really meant it. After all, it had been at least three hours since the Tooth and Claw disaster. He would have been glad to see anyone.

Malik nodded to Grandpa. "It's nice to see you again, Mr. Malone," he said.

"You've been here?" I asked Grandpa. "The whole time?"

Grandpa twisted the thing in his hands some more, and I noticed it was one of the fish castles from the pet store. I knew he hadn't paid for it, but I didn't think it was the right time to mention it. "It wasn't really that long to wait," Grandpa said.

"Why didn't you just go home?" I blurted. "It's not that far."

"Well, that's the funny thing," Grandpa said, only he didn't sound like it was funny at all. "I couldn't quite remember the streets to take. But don't tell your mother that, okay?"

It was the first time he'd ever admitted that he needed help. "I have a feeling she already knows, Grandpa," I told him. "We better get home."

We walked home slowly. Grandpa kept holding his hip, and his face seemed to have more creases than before. Still, he tried to keep up a conversation with Malik and me.

"I would've headed home," he was telling Malik. "But this is a new subdivision to me. All the houses look alike."

We were passing a two-story house that looked like a barn. The one before it was a ranch. I didn't bother to point out to Grandpa that they were very different because it wouldn't have done any good. I knew exactly what Grandpa was doing. Making excuses. Or as Dad would say, telling a lie.

Malik nodded as if he believed every word Grandpa said. "I remember getting lost when I went to visit my dad right after he moved away," he said.

"What did you do?" Grandpa asked.

It surprised me that Malik had never told me this story. I thought he told me everything. "Dad found me," Malik admitted. "But after that, I made sure to always remember my way."

"How do you do that?" Grandpa asked.

"Well, first, I try to find things that look out of the ordinary. Like that tree," Malik said, pointing to a withered trunk. "It looks like a bony old witch."

"Yes. Yes, it does," Grandpa said with a laugh. "There's the crooked nose, and the dead branches are the old hag's hair."

I squinted at the tree. I didn't see a witch. All I saw

was an old tree that needed to be chopped down.

"Then I stare at it until it becomes a picture in my brain," Malik continued as we stopped in front of his house. "Sort of like taking a photograph with my eyes."

"A picture!" Grandpa said. "Clever idea. Let me try."

Grandpa stood in front of Malik's house and stared. Then he held up his hands, pretending to hold a camera. "Snap!" he said with a flick of the pretend-camera button. "Yep. That ought to do it. Thanks for the tip."

We waited until Malik went inside his house, then Grandpa and I headed for home. Grandpa had his hands in front of his face, pointing his make-believe camera the entire time. Thanks to Malik, my grandfather was walking down the street looking like a complete fool, but I had to admit, pictures did seem like a good idea. I tried to stay in the shadows and glanced at windows, praying nobody was watching my grandfather playing pretend.

"Click!" he said when we passed an old truck with a rusted bumper. It was so dark that the streetlights had popped on. The truck looked like it was lit up with spotlights.

"Click!" he said when he saw the street sign marking the corner at Briggs. "That's our street, Charlie. I'll remember that."

As soon as we turned the corner I knew something was wrong. Very wrong. A police car was parked in our driveway, the red and blue lights flashing like fireworks on the Fourth of July.

Neighbors were clustered in the yard. A policewoman stood on the porch talking to my parents, but when Mom saw us coming up the sidewalk she pushed the officer out of the way. "There he is!" she screamed.

"Yeah," I said, holding my shoulders straight. "I found him."

But Mom didn't run to Grandpa. It was me she headed for. "Where have you been?" she asked, pulling away after nearly tackling me with a smothering hug.

I tried to tell her but she had squeezed all the air out of me. And then both Mom and Dad started talking, one right after the other, so it was impossible to squeeze in a word.

First Mom: I told you to stay in the house.

Then Dad: With the doors locked!

Mom again: It's bad enough we had to worry about your grandfather.

Followed by Dad: You let us down, Logan.

Mom once more: We had no idea where you were.

Dad again: You didn't even leave a note.

"Anything could've happened to you!" Mom said. "What did you expect us to think?"

"I expected you to be glad I found Grandpa," I muttered.

Mom gave me another nose-crushing hug. "Of course we're glad you found your grandfather," she said. "It's just that we were so worried about you."

Dad reached over and squeezed my shoulder. "You could've called us on our cell phone," he said. "We have to be able to trust you to make responsible decisions, Logan. All the time."

I couldn't believe it. Instead of being a hero, I had landed, smack-dab, in trouble again.

Grandpa aimed his imaginary camera at us and took another pretend picture.

"What is he doing?" Mom asked.

I grabbed her elbow and pulled her toward the house. "We have got to talk," I told Mom and Dad. "I have an idea."

Grandpa didn't suspect a thing when Dad pulled into the Buy-A-Lot discount store parking lot the next afternoon. "Just to pick up a few things," Mom said with a slight smile. Once inside, we didn't stop until we reached the electronics section near the back of the store.

"There," I said. "It's exactly what you need."

Grandpa's eyes flitted over the shelves to find what I meant. Cameras.

"A real camera," I said. "You can store the pictures on the camera and then transfer them to my computer. You'll be able to keep files and files of pictures."

I wanted to add that he wouldn't look stupid taking real pictures, but I kept that part to myself.

"Can I print pictures, too?" Grandpa asked.

I was about to argue that printing pictures would be too expensive, but then I remembered all those sticky notes on his walls and thought about what they would look like with tiny pictures next to them. Instead of arguing, I nodded. "We could print some of them," I said.

Grandpa pulled a camera off the hook. The smile seemed to drain off his face. "These are expensive, Charlie. Very expensive."

That's when Mom pulled a wad of money out of her pocket. "We all chipped in," she said.

"Even Logan," Dad said. "He donated all his birthday money. It was his idea!"

"We want you to have this," I said.

For the rest of the day, Grandpa took pictures of everyone doing everything. It was starting to get on my nerves, because he always seemed to catch me when I wasn't expecting it. Mom and Dad didn't seem to mind. They would pose as if every picture was going to be framed and hung on a museum wall.

"See," I heard Dad tell her. "Everything is working out. You just needed to give it a little more time."

Mom reached up for the kiss Dad was offering just as Grandpa took a picture, but I noticed Mom didn't say anything, and I wondered what Dad had meant.

I was in the middle of brushing my teeth on Monday morning when Mom's bloodcurdling scream brought me running from the bathroom.

Dad and I rushed to the kitchen at the same time. Mom's hands covered her mouth, and her purse was on the floor. She stared at it as if it were something oozing out of the toilet. "This is the *last straw*! Get them out of there," she hissed. "Get them out *now*."

Just then, Grandpa strolled into the kitchen, camera in hand.

"Anybody see my chompers?" he asked.

When I pulled Grandpa's teeth out of Mom's purse I laughed, showering my chin with toothpaste. Even Dad was smiling.

"It is *not* funny," Mom said. She looked at Dad like it was partly his fault. "I have *had* it!"

"It's only teeth," Dad said softly. I noticed he wasn't smiling anymore. "Not the end of the world."

Grandpa losing his teeth had almost become a morning ritual. I don't know why Mom was making such a big deal out of it, but what Grandpa did next wasn't funny at all.

He snapped a picture of me, standing in my underwear with my toothbrush sticking out of my mouth. I was holding Mom's purse in one hand and Grandpa's teeth in the other.

"Stop that," I mumbled around my toothbrush. I shoved his dentures into his hand as if they were a time bomb.

"But Charlie—"

"My name is LOGAN! Can't you remember just once!"

Grandpa stood there, camera in one hand and dentures in the other. A deep crease between his eyes pinched his eyebrows into a worried arch.

I knew I shouldn't have yelled, but I was in a hurry. I almost stopped to apologize, but kept going instead. After all, he was the one that was causing everyone to be late. Not me.

16

Fighting Mad

Malik was waiting on the playground, just like always.

"Thanks for your help the other day," I told Malik.

Malik shrugged like it was no big deal and then bent over to root around for something in the bottom of his enormous backpack. "Forget it."

I had already tried, but it was etched in my brain like one of those pretend pictures Grandpa kept taking. "I can't," I said. "Not when my Dad is making me spend every afternoon working, and it's all thanks to the mess Grandpa and Emily made of everything."

I explained what had happened when Grandpa opened the rat cage. "I have to scoop poop every afternoon at the pet store to help pay back what was broken," I finished.

"You mean you got a job?" Malik asked. He made it sound like I had just won the lottery. He stood up so fast his glasses slid halfway down on his nose. "Your parents are actually letting you work?"

I made my voice as hard as a Doberman's toenails. "They're not letting me work. They're *making* me. I don't get a red cent for it, either. I have to work to pay for everything that got smashed. What's even worse is that I spent all my birthday money on a camera for Grandpa. I am now officially broke!"

Malik pushed the glasses back up on his nose. "But you get to hang out at the pet store," he said. "You like the pet store."

It was just like Malik to find something good in a hopeless situation. "If Emily keeps up her attack plan, I'll never get enough stupid smiley faces to earn a pet," I pointed out. "So what does it matter?"

Malik slapped me on the shoulder. "Sure you will. Just pretend that Emily Scott doesn't exist and you'll have it made."

"Impossible," I groaned.

"Nothing is impossible," Malik pointed out. "You only have to outlast her for two weeks. You can do *anything* for two weeks."

I took a deep breath and faced the doors of Dooley Elementary. Two weeks seemed like an eternity.

"It won't be as bad as you think," Malik added.

He was right. It wasn't as bad as I thought it would be.

It was worse.

I tried Malik's advice and ignored Emily on the way to my desk, but there, dead center, was a picture of a rat with my name printed across it. I felt my face get hot, and my ears felt like they were dipped in dragon snot.

Emily stood there, a smile plastered across her face. When Sharissa and Barbara saw the picture they giggled.

"I can't believe you're talking to Ratfink," Sharissa said to Malik.

"After all, he told everyone you keep poop in your pack," Barbara added.

I had to hand it to my best friend. For a bookworm, he had a lot of spunk, because the next thing he did was look right at Emily. "That was just one of Logan's stories," he said to her. "Were you dumb enough to really believe it?"

Everyone knew by now that Emily thought she was smarter than anyone. She looked like a snake ready to strike when she squared her shoulders and leaned close to Malik. "Of course I didn't," she said. "And I'm smart enough to find out what you've got hidden in there."

Malik shrugged. When he did, the pack on his shoulder slid to the floor and landed right on Emily's toe.

Despite my curiosity about what Malik had buried in his pack, I didn't want to find out by having Emily announce it to the world. When she turned and walked away, I hoped her foot hurt with every step. I took a deep breath and tore the rat picture off my desk, wadded it up into a tight ball, and tossed it in the trash can. Then I gritted my teeth and started pretending that Emily Scott was as extinct as the bloodthirsty T. rex she reminded me of.

That afternoon, when Mr. Simon handed out the timed math test, he stopped by the side of my desk long enough to pat me on the shoulder. "You're having a good day, Logan," he said. I smiled and sat up just a bit taller. I glanced at the clock. Another thirty minutes and I would have my first good report to take home.

Mr. Simon twirled the dial of the egg timer in his

hand. "Go!" he told the class as if he were starting an Olympic relay race.

I bent over my paper. The scratching of pencils on paper nearly drowned out the tick-tick-tick of the timer.

I had studied all the way to twelve times twelve. I knew them. Really I did. But as soon as that timer started, my brain froze like penguin snot. I tapped my foot in time to the ticking until the numbers started making sense.

The first row wasn't too bad. I only had to skip one. The second row started out okay, but the middle row stumped me with nine times seven. I tried counting it out on my fingers, but that was taking too long. I chewed off the tip of my eraser as I tried to work up from one I knew, but I couldn't think over the tick-tick-tick of the timer. I heard Malik and Emily slam their pencils down at the same time to show they were done. There was no way I would finish. I glanced up to see how much time was left. That's when Emily made her move.

"Stop copying," she said loud enough to measure 9.9 on the Richter scale.

Mr. Simon looked up from a pile of papers he was grading. "Is there a problem, Emily?" he asked.

"He's cheating," she announced. Then Emily pointed right at me.

"I saw him, too," Sharissa said.

"Mr. Malone," Mr. Simon said before I could start to answer. "Tear up your paper and throw it in the trash. Then bring me your agenda."

"But . . ."

"NOW," he said in a voice that meant there was no use explaining.

I heard Sharissa and Barbara giggle when I threw away my math test. I knew a fat red zero would go in Mr. Simon's grade book by my name. Even worse was the huge red frowning face he drew at the bottom of my agenda.

"I'm disappointed, Logan," Mr. Simon said. "Very disappointed."

I wasn't disappointed. I was mad. Fighting mad.

"I need your help," I told Malik on my way to the Tooth and Claw that afternoon.

Malik nodded. "I was wondering when you would ask," he said. "Multiplication is a simple system of re-peated addition. Once you understand that, all you have to do is memorize the facts."

"What are you talking about?" I asked.

"Multiplication. It's just adding over and over again," he said.

I shook my head. "Why are you telling me about multiplication?"

Blink, blink. Blink. Malik stared at me. "You asked me for my help, so I'm helping you," Malik said.

"No, no, no," I said. "I don't need help with math."

"Yes you do."

"Okay, I do need help with math. But the problem I have right now can't be solved with multiplication." Then I told Malik my plan for getting even with Emily. It had come to me in a moment of true inspiration when Mr. Simon made me march up to his desk. Sharissa and Barbara had reacted in their all-too-familiar way. With giggles. I had learned to hate the sound. It reminded me of flaming arrows aimed right at my heart. I wanted to use a shield to bounce them back at Emily instead. That's when my plan came to me.

"I'm going to give her a dose of her own medicine," I explained. "To do that, I need you to do what you do best."

I knew by the way Malik's eyes were blinking a mile a minute that he wasn't convinced. "Trust me," I said with my hand on his shoulder. "There is no way this can backfire. Besides, aren't you tired of her pestering you about your pack? She deserves this and you know it."

That's all it took. I knew that while I was scooping cat litter, Malik would be concocting a special revenge potion with his science kit.

17

Keeper

When I pushed open the door to the Tooth and Claw, Mitchell looked at me as if I was something a cat hacked up. He didn't talk to me and I didn't talk to him. I didn't have time anyway. Mrs. Harrison was there to show me what she expected me to do, and she expected a lot.

I was to scoop out litter boxes in the kitten kennels, change the papers in the birdcages, and spread fresh cedar chips for the hamsters, gerbils, and rats. I planned to save the rats for last. I also was responsible for setting up new cages for the hamsters that kids kept bringing into the store.

A few years back Mrs. Harrison had made a mistake when a kid brought in a litter of hamsters he didn't want. She agreed to try and sell them. Ever since then, shoeboxes of hamsters kept appearing on the counter. Kids would come in, drop the box on the counter, and run.

That afternoon, two boxes showed up. Mrs. Harrison stood at the counter and peered inside. "This is getting out of hand," she said.

There were a total of seven new hamsters crawling around inside the boxes. "Isn't this the opposite of what's supposed to be happening in a pet store?" I asked. "I mean, how can you make money if kids keep *giving* you hamsters instead of *buying* them?"

Mrs. Harrison tapped the counter with her fingernail. "You have a future ahead of you, Logan. Someday you'll be making more money than me."

"Can't you just tell them to stop bringing the hamsters in?" I asked.

"I could," she said, "but then what would happen to the hamsters?"

"There must be a better idea," I said as Mrs. Harrison slipped on a jacket and got ready to leave.

"If you think of something," Mrs. Harrison said, "be sure to let me know."

As soon as she left I went to work. I was in the middle of scooping litter boxes when the bells over the door jangled. I looked up, and there he was.

Grandpa.

"Click!" Grandpa snapped a picture of me holding a scoop full of dirty litter.

"How did you find me?" I asked.

"No problem," he said, patting his shirt pocket where a folded map stuck out. "I picked up a map and studied the area. Now I know my way around like I know the back of my hand. Been taking pictures like your friend suggested, too. The problem is solved."

I turned away from him and marched up to the counter to take care of the hamsters.

"You keep hamsters in boxes?" Grandpa asked as he followed me.

"Of course we don't," I said. I quickly told him about Mrs. Harrison's hamster dilemma as I let a couple of them take turns in plastic exercise balls.

I wondered if hamsters actually liked being trapped in the big plastic balls. They ran and ran and ran, sending the ball rolling across the floor. I felt sort of sorry for them. No matter how hard their legs worked, they could never get out of that ball.

"It's like they're racing," Grandpa said. "Maybe that's what you should do. Have hamster races, and the winner gets to go home with somebody!"

I couldn't help but laugh at the thought of hamsters winning prizes. "That sounds like something you'd read in a book," I told Grandpa.

"You could write that story," Grandpa said. "You're good at writing."

"No, I'm not," I said. "I just tell stories."

For a brief moment, that look of total confusion crossed Grandpa's face. I was afraid he was going to start squawking like a bird again, but I was surprised when he just asked, "Isn't that what a book is? A story written down? You could write a good story about hamsters, Charlie. I just know it."

"But it was your idea," I pointed out.

"I'm not the writer. You are," Grandpa said.

It was the first time anyone had ever admitted that my storytelling had some potential, and while I cleaned up the droppings splattered beneath the parrot's perch, I imagined writing a story where hamsters ran races like in the Kentucky Derby horse race.

While the hamsters ran around and I prepared their cages, Grandpa flipped through magazines. Every once in a while a hamster ball would run into his shoe. Grandpa would turn it so the hamster could race in the other direction.

"Look at this, Charlie," Grandpa said, tapping the open page of a magazine.

The Tooth and Claw had a shelf full of magazines with articles about all kinds of animals. There were stories about ferrets, reptiles, pigs, goats, and even llamas. I was pretty sure my mom would draw the line at llamas, even though they were supposed to be nice and gentle, which surprised me.

I glanced at the page Grandpa was studying. "Imagine that," he said. "A monkey was trained to help a fella in a wheelchair."

"Monkeys can also tear the skin off your nose," I muttered, remembering an article that was in the newspaper not too long ago.

"True, true," Grandpa said. "Monkeys can be dangerous, but it says here that other animals have been trained as companions. Here's something about a parrot that dials 911 in case of an emergency."

"Bet the place is a mess," I said. I had just found out the hard way that birds weren't particular where they splattered.

"They've had great success with dogs that sense seizures before they even happen," Grandpa continued.

I looked over Grandpa's arm so I could see the picture. A small dog with long yellow hair leaned against the leg of a girl about my age. The girl's hand rested lightly on the dog's head. "What good does sensing seizures do?" I asked. "It's not like the dog can stop them from coming."

"According to this, the dog gets her to a secure place so she won't get hurt," Grandpa said. "Keeps her safe. Seems like a good thing to me. That's worth remembering."

To prove his point, Grandpa propped the open magazine on the shelf and took a picture of the page just as Mitchell walked by.

I told myself that there was nothing wrong with a grandfather taking real pictures, but by the time I had finished feeding the rabbits I was getting fed up with Grandpa and his camera. "Do you have to take a picture of *everything*?" I asked. "You'll just have to erase most of them."

"I can't erase them," Grandpa said, as if I had told him he should pluck out his eyeballs and feed them to a flock of vultures.

"If you don't, your camera will run out of memory," I pointed out.

"Run out of memory." Grandpa said each word as if he could taste them, and I knew he was thinking about his own brain running out of memories. The sticky notes plastered on his wall and the notebook by his bed flashed through my mind.

"You don't have to get rid of them for good," I explained a little more patiently. "We could store some of them on my computer."

"I'd appreciate that," Grandpa said. "I really don't want to run out of memory."

Later that night, Grandpa knocked on my bedroom door. "My camera says it's full," Grandpa said. "Would you mind showing me how to save my memories? Can you do that, Charlie?"

I closed my math book. Anything was better than finding the area and perimeter of a page full of shapes. I plugged Grandpa's camera into my computer, and we watched the picture files copy. Then I showed Grandpa how to view all the shots, one right after the other. I sat beside him, watching. The pictures flashed by like a movie in slow motion.

If it had been me, I would have erased all of them, but I showed him how to create files on the computer so he could organize pictures by categories on my hard drive.

Grandpa glanced at how I had my files. Games. Friends. Homework. "Where are your stories, Charlie? What file are they in?"

It occurred to me that I was blinking in confusion just like Malik would do. "What do you mean?"

"If you're going to be a writer, don't you have to have files for your ideas? Like the one about hamsters winning races. Where is that one?"

Grandpa refused to do another thing until I had created a file for stories and added the idea about hamsters racing. Grandpa added a few more ideas, which even I had to admit were funny. After we had done that, I picked up his camera to remind him why he had come to my room in the first place.

"Now you see how we can save your pictures on my computer, and you can just delete all of them from the camera," I told him.

"I can't do that," Grandpa said. "I need some of them."

"Why do you need a picture of the house on the corner?" I asked as we slowly went through the pictures to decide which ones to delete.

Grandpa didn't look at me when he answered. His words came slowly, and I had to listen hard just to hear them. "That's where I turn," he said. "To get back here."

"But why keep this shot of Mom in her robe?"

"Your grandmother gave your mother that robe,"

Grandpa said. "The last Christmas we had together. I remember how she picked out that one because she thought it would bring out the color in your mother's eyes. I like that memory."

That's when it hit me. The pictures in his camera were helping him practice his memories the same way the sticky notes and the notebook full of lists did. I flipped back through the other pictures he was keeping on his camera. Ones of Mom, Dad, the house. Shots of the neighborhood and the Tooth and Claw. Then I found the one showing me standing in my underwear with my toothbrush sticking out of my mouth, holding Grandpa's dentures in one hand and Mom's purse in the other. "This one *has* to go," I argued.

"Never," Grandpa said.

"But I'm in my . . . underwear!" I whispered the last word even though it was only Grandpa and me in my room.

"So what?" Grandpa said as he snatched the camera out of my hands. "It's my camera, and I'll decide which pictures are keepers. And that, my boy, is a *keeper*!"

"What if someone sees it?" I asked. "It would be the end of the world as I know it if someone sees that picture of me in my underwear and holding a woman's purse."

"Nonsense," Grandpa said. "There are worse things than being laughed at, you know. Besides, no one but me will ever see this."

"You're a real pain, you know that?" I blurted.

When Grandpa had first come to live with us, I wouldn't have dreamed of saying something so honest. Now that he had followed me around for weeks, it was just like talking to Malik. Mom would have grounded me for eternity if she had heard me. Grandpa, on the other hand, acted like it didn't bother him one bit.

"Remember, Charlie. Your mother says you take after me," he said with a grin as he left my room.

"I am NOT like you!" I shouted, but Grandpa didn't hear me. He had already closed my door.

18

Turnabout, Fair Play?

I was out of breath by the time I reached school the next morning. Malik was on the playground, his backpack on the ground by his sneakers. I pointed at the straining zipper. "Do you have it?" I asked my best friend.

Malik nodded. "But before I hand it over, I want you to be sure. Is this really a good idea?"

I glanced at the top of the steps leading into Dooley Elementary. Emily was talking to Sharissa and Barbara, their heads close together so they could whisper. One of Sharissa's high-pitched laughs echoed across the playground. I could see that flaming arrow heading straight at me. I wondered if I could convince my parents to let me get one of those dogs that could sense seizures. Only instead of seizures, I would train it to detect giggles so it could warn me in time to run as far away as possible. Of course, I couldn't think about a pet until I had ten smiling reports from Mr. Simon, and that wasn't going to happen until I took care of Emily once and for all.

"I have never been more sure of anything in my life," I told Malik through clenched teeth. "I have to strike before Emily thinks of something else to get me in trouble."

Malik looked at Emily. Then he looked at me. "Don't blame me if it doesn't work," he said. He dug deep in his backpack and pulled out a small plastic pill bottle, but I knew there was no medicine inside.

I flicked open the lid. One sniff and tears puddled in my eyes. It smelled like a mixture of skunk, rotten eggs, and boiled cabbage. Perfect.

I recapped the bottle and slipped it into my pocket. I needed the perfect time to unleash my revenge potion. It was hard to concentrate on spelling. It was next to impossible to pay attention in social stud-ies. Finally the perfect moment arrived. Mr. Simon had collected all the morning work. Our desks were cleared. I knew what was coming.

"Line up for lunch," Mr. Simon said.

I flicked the lid off the bottle and tipped it under Emily's desk on my way to line up.

It didn't take long.

"PHEEE-YEWWWW!" Sharissa yelped.

"What's that smell?" Barbara asked.

Half the class was already pinching their noses. It was now or never.

I jabbed Randy and pointed at Emily. That's all it took.

"It's Emily," Randy announced. "She farted."

My plan had worked perfectly. I didn't have to say a word.

"Ew, yuck," Sharissa said, and moved as far away from Emily as she could get.

Someone blew on their arm, making a long wet raspberry.

Emily's face was as red as a baboon's butt. There was something else I saw. Something I never imag-ined seeing on Emily the Snot's face.

Tears.

Oh yeah. One other thing I noticed. Somebody else wasn't laughing.

Mr. Simon.

At lunch, Emily sat by herself at the end of the table, staring at the noodles in her chili as if they were worms. The seats nearest her were empty.

"Chili's the last thing *you* need," Randy said to her as he walked past.

"Beans, beans, good for the heart," Bobby sang.

"The more you eat, the more you FART!" finished the kids at the end of the table.

Emily's cheeks were splotched with red. Emily was getting a big taste of what she dished out on a regular basis. I should have been happy, but I wasn't. I had been on the receiving end of her teasing long enough to know how she was feeling. Now I was on the other side, and being on the other side wasn't all it was cracked up to be. Sometimes, I thought, it would be good to have my grandfather's memory problem. Then I could forget things I wanted to forget. Like the way my stomach didn't feel so good when Randy blew a wet raspberry on the skin of his arm for the umpteenth time.

No matter how hard he had tried, Mr. Simon wasn't able to blame me for a single thing, but I didn't feel all that good about the smiley face sketched in my agenda at the end of the day. I stuffed the notebook in my pack and headed out the door.

"Wait up!" Malik yelled down the hall. "I'll walk with you."

Malik slung his pack over his right shoulder and hurried to catch up. When we reached the front door, Emily was waiting at the top of the steps.

"Here comes the class poop head with his trusty poop-pack," Emily said so everyone could hear, but today was different. Today she was by herself. No one else seemed interested in Malik's pack.

"You're the one stinking up the classroom," Malik blurted. "Not me!"

I knew Malik felt good, finally getting a jab in at Emily, but I was in no mood for a fight.

Emily's eyes narrowed, and she had her hands on her hips. *"You!"* she said. *"You're* the one that did it."

Malik smiled and shook his head. "I did nothing in class today," he said. "Nothing at all."

He was telling the truth. Malik might have worked all night with his science kit to make the smelly concoction, but he hadn't done a thing in the classroom. That was all my doing.

Emily turned her killer gaze on me. "Then it was *you,* wasn't it?"

"I'm late," I said, and shouldered past her.

"Besides," Malik said, "turnabout is fair play!"

I jerked on Malik's backpack and pulled him down the steps before he said another word.

As we walked down the steps, I couldn't help but hear Emily's final words. "Just wait," she warned. "You'll be sorry. Very sorry."

What she didn't realize was that I already felt sorry. Of course, I could never admit that to anyone.

Earning smiling reports seemed to get easier after that. It helped that Mr. Simon could sense trouble the way a shark smells blood. Even Emily had to keep an eye out for him. By Thursday, everyone seemed to have forgotten about Emily's stinky fart. Mostly it was because we were all excited about something else.

The fall carnival.

The carnival was a big Dooley Elementary tradition. Every class organized an event. The class got to decide how to use the money that was raised. Mr. Simon divided us into groups and told us our job was to come up with an idea. The following day each group would present their plan to the class and then we'd vote. Our idea had to be original, safe, cost-effective, and have the potential to earn money.

Mr. Simon was not the kind of teacher who let us

pick our own partners, so we had to wait for him to divide us into groups. He dragged it out the way our preacher drags out the sermon on Christmas morning. An involuntary cheer escaped my lips when Mr. Simon called my name for Malik's group. The cheer quickly turned to a groan when he also called Emily's name. I couldn't believe it. Malik, me, and Emily, the Snot, Scott all in the same group. Was there no justice in the universe?

Randy and Jessica rounded off our group. "Let's get down to business," I said as soon as we met in the back corner of the room. "I want to have the winning idea."

Randy and Jessica sat cross-legged across from Malik and me. Malik leaned against his backpack. Emily scooted up until she was almost in the middle of our little circle.

"I know," Emily said with a toothy smile. "We could raffle off tickets."

"Tickets to what?" Randy asked as if Emily really had a good idea.

"The winner would get to look inside Malik's backpack," she said. Then she laughed at her own joke.

Blink, blink. Blink. Malik didn't say a word. He didn't need to. His fluttering eyes said enough.

My toes twitched inside my sneakers, tempted to kick Emily right then and there. But then a big frowning face flashed before my eyes, so I said instead, "This is important. We don't have time for fighting."

Emily opened her mouth as if she was ready to shoot out words as fast as a pitching machine. Instead, she snapped her mouth shut and looked at me for a solid fifteen seconds. "You're right," she finally said.

"I am?" I asked, embarrassed that my voice cracked when I said it.

Emily nodded. "I want our group to have the winning idea, too. The only way to do that is to work together. Agreed?"

Emily looked at me and waited. "Agreed," I said.

Then she actually looked at Malik. "I call a truce," she told him. "For now. Agreed?"

"Agreed," he said.

And then we got down to work.

It felt good not having to worry about contriving insults or pranks. We could fully concentrate on our ideas for the carnival. Of course, that didn't mean we had any luck in that department.

"What about a dunking booth?" Emily suggested. "Soaking people would be cheap and popular."

"Mrs. Ramsey's third grade does that every year," Jessica pointed out.

I almost opened my mouth to tell Emily how stupid her idea was, but then I realized that she wouldn't have known about Mrs. Ramsey's class tradition, since she was new.

"The duck-shooting booth was a big hit a few years ago," Bobby said.

"Some of the mothers didn't like kids shooting guns," David remembered. "Even though they were pretend."

"I hate the idea of shooting animals," Emily added. "Even if they are plastic."

That surprised me. I thought Emily was mean to every creature on Earth, living or dead.

Bake sale. Cake walk. Baseball card auction. There was something wrong with every idea.

On Friday, before lunch, Mr. Simon gave the carnival teams extra time to put finishing touches on their plans before presenting ideas. Our team was clueless. In fifteen minutes he was going to ask what we had come up with, and we had nothing.

Zero.

Zilch.

Nada.

"We can't stand up there and admit our team is clueless," Emily said.

I found myself agreeing with her. "We have all the brains and all the talent," I added. "There has to be *something* we can do." My thoughts kept twisting and turning. They were all jumbled up, as if they had been tumbling in one of those hamster wheels at the Tooth and Claw.

The hamsters. What was it that Grandpa had said? Something about letting hamsters race for a home?

"I've got it!" I yelped. Mr. Simon glanced up from the papers he was grading. I lowered my voice and told my team the idea.

"It just might work," Malik said slowly.

"It's definitely clever," Jessica asked. "Nobody has ever thought up anything like that before."

"And it would help the community," Randy added. "Plus, I bet lots of kids would pay money to do it."

We all looked at Emily, waiting for her to nix the idea. She surprised everyone, me most of all.

"I think it's a great idea, Logan," she said. "Let's flesh out the details so we can sell it to the class!" Emily was down on her hands and knees, already sketching a poster to use for the presentation.

at afternoon, I waved goodbye to Malik and
inside the Tooth and Claw after school. I had
ed four days of Mr. Simon's smiling reign of
. Not only that, I was the star in my class. I
d have felt good, but I didn't.

soon as I opened the door to the pet store, I re-
ered the way Grandpa had leaned against the
zine rack, reading articles, and how he would
over and send the hamsters rolling in another
tion whenever one had bumped into his shoe.
's when it hit me. I had taken all the credit, but
riginal idea wasn't really mine. It was Grandpa's.
sn't about to admit that to anyone. Especially
y.

he big rat stretched his nose in my direction when
him, his beady eyes locked on mine as if he knew
I was thinking. The rat's whiskers twitched like
anted to say something.

ou don't know anything," I told it. "You're just
"

ut the real truth was, at that very moment, I felt
he biggest rat of them all.

We put our heads together and worked out the details while Emily wrote them down. Even I had to
admit the little pictures of hamsters she added were
good. We finished just as the timer on Mr. Simon's
desk dinged.

The first group to present their idea suggested we
do face painting. "Kids will pay to have flowers and
stuff painted on their cheeks," they explained.

Another group wanted to organize a booth where
people could sell unwanted toys. "It would be like
a garage sale," they said. I thought that was pretty
good, but not as good as ours.

The third group wanted our class to arrange a talent show. "Everyone likes to show off," they said, but
they hadn't figured out how we would earn lots of
money from a talent show.

Then it was our turn. We had all voted for Malik
to do the talking. Even Emily. If anyone was going
to persuade Mr. Simon that our idea was the best, it
would be the brain of the class. Malik didn't let us
down. He stood before the class and began talking as
if he were the president giving a speech.

"Unwanted pets," Malik said. "It's a problem not
only for our community, but for the poor animals
themselves." Malik nodded in my direction. "Thanks

to Logan, who did exceptional firsthand research, we have determined that unwanted pets are a serious problem."

"We all worked on it," Emily blurted, but for once Mr. Simon didn't take her side.

"You chose Malik to present your idea," he said. "Let him finish."

The tips of her ears turned red, but she closed her mouth and slouched back down in her chair. It was obviously hard for her to let someone else be center stage. I felt kind of sorry for her. But only for a split second.

Malik was using ten-dollar words, making it sound like we had been working on this idea all along. Even I was impressed.

"Our solution to this complex problem will not only help the animals, but it will also earn more money than any other booths at the fair," Malik said with such certainty that even Sharissa and Barbara looked halfway convinced. "We propose The First Annual Dooley Elementary Hamster Derby Races," Malik announced. "We'll earn money by having kids pay entrance fees. Kids will race one another, and the ones that come in first, second, and third in each race will win a hamster. It's like the cakewalk, only better,

because kids get to run races chair."

"But why would they pay to could just go to the store and rissa asked.

"The same reason someon cakewalk when they could ju Malik pointed out with a smile

"Only nobody has ever tho before," I added. And then I couldn't resist. "My idea is orig

"*Our* idea," Emily blurted, busy talking that nobody heard

"It certainly is unique," M nod. "And it could earn mone Mrs. Harrison would donate th

Then everyone was talking a whose idea was the winner. Mi

Maybe it wasn't fair to take ter all, it was my idea to begin helped make it sound good. Al a poster. I really didn't see wh to be so mad, but it was obviou of lunch, Emily sat by herself a glaring in my direction.

19

Bathrobe Burglar

That night, just before bed, I went downstairs for a glass of milk, but as soon as I saw the front door standing wide open, I galloped back upstairs.

"BURGLARS!" I screamed as I shoved open my parents' bedroom door. "There are burglars in the house!"

Dad flew out of the bathroom and Mom jumped out of bed. "This better not be one of your stories," Dad warned.

"It's true," I told him. "The front door is wide open."

Dad and Mom hurried out in the hall. "Wait here," Mom said.

There was no way I was going to stay by myself. I tiptoed down the stairs after them and crouched on the third step from the bottom. I figured the steps were the safest place to be. I was ready to sprint outside if the burglar appeared at the top of the steps and just as ready to hightail it to my room and slam the door if the threat came from below.

As soon as Dad saw the open door, he flipped the switch, flooding the front yard with lights, and stepped outside.

"I'll call the police," Mom yelled, running toward the kitchen phone.

"Wait!" Dad called from the front porch.

His words brought Mom to a skidding stop.

I didn't hear any screams. There were no gunshots or scary thumps. Instead, I heard voices. They were soft and low, as if whoever was talking didn't want to be heard. Then there were footsteps on the stairs. A dark shadow blocked the light from the porch for a brief moment before someone stepped through the open door.

I wouldn't have been surprised to see a hulking man wearing a black mask. Or maybe a crazed drug addict with red eyes and torn jeans. Even an alien from outer space with tentacles and twenty-three eyeballs wouldn't have been as shocking as what came through the door at that very moment.

The first thing I saw was a bare foot at the bottom of a very skinny leg. Then I saw a flash of blue. A blue I knew too well. The blue of Mom's bathrobe.

I was pretty sure Dr. Phil would not approve of a ten-year-old seeing his grandfather coming through the front door wearing his mother's robe. Especially since the robe didn't quite go all the way around him. I thought about telling Mom that, but when I looked at her eyes I knew better than to make a sound. Her eyes were no longer wide. Now they were squinty. Her mouth was set in a line, and she crossed her arms over her chest.

"I came up from the basement for something," Grandpa was saying as Dad slowly eased him inside.

"Then I thought a bit of fresh air would be nice," Grandpa continued, his voice hoarse and ragged as if his throat were swollen.

"You went outside in a robe?" Mom asked. "*My* robe?"

Grandpa looked down at the blue sash tied at his waist. He tried to pull it tighter, but he was just too big and the robe was way too small. I tried not to notice the blue veins etched on his thighs. "I couldn't find mine," Grandpa explained. His fingers plucked at the end of the belt. "This was in the clothes basket in the utility room. I didn't think you'd mind. It was only going to be for a minute."

Dad rested his hand on Grandpa's shoulder. "It's okay," he said. "Joyce doesn't mind."

Mom glared at Dad.

"Let's go on to bed," Dad said. "It's late."

"Yes," Grandpa said as they started downstairs to the basement. "I'm tired. Very tired. I think bed is a good idea."

It had been a while since Grandpa had had a really bad day. I had almost forgotten how bad they could be. From the expression on Mom's face, I could tell she had forgotten, too.

"I guess it's easy to get turned around when it's so dark," I said, hoping it would help erase the hard look that had settled into Mom's eyes. "I bet Grandpa was scared. It's a good thing we found him before he got too lost."

But Mom didn't answer me. She was already heading upstairs to bed.

It was hard getting to sleep that night. Every time I closed my eyes I saw Grandpa wearing Mom's robe. I was in the middle of imagining all the jokes Emily would tell everyone if she had seen it when I heard Mom and Dad talking from across the hall. It was a quiet night, and their voices were louder than usual, so I could hear them if I sat on the floor by the door and listened really hard. At first I was worried that they were talking about me, but I was surprised to figure out they were talking about Grandpa instead.

Mom's voice was firm: I have a list of places. It won't hurt to look at a few.

Dad didn't sound happy: I'm not kicking my father out of the house.

Mom wasn't backing down: These places are equipped to deal with patients like him.

Dad was getting louder: Just because he forgets things every once in a while, it does not mean he needs to be locked away.

Mom matched Dad's voice. "I'm not talking about locking him up. But he went for a walk in my robe, for crying out loud. Logan was right. If we hadn't found him he could've been lost all night. It's only going to get worse. You have to face that. It's not fair that you expect Logan—and me—to look after him. Please. I'm only asking that we look."

There was a long silence after that. I thought maybe they were so mad they had stopped talking to each other. But then I heard some murmurs. Too quiet for me to understand.

I crawled back in bed and pulled up the covers. I had gotten used to Grandpa. His quirks had become part of my everyday life. I knew Mom hadn't been crazy about having Grandpa move in, but I thought she'd gotten used to it. Now I knew the truth. But I couldn't believe that Mom had used things I had said to try and convince Dad that Grandpa should be living in some sort of assisted living apartment. I didn't think Mom ever listened to me.

I lay in bed and thought about everything that had happened since Grandpa moved in with us. All the things I had said and done. Just because I complained about Grandpa and worried that he might embarrass me didn't really make it my fault that Mom wanted to ship him off. After all, it was Grandpa and the things he did that Mom was upset about. Right?

Wondering kept me awake for a long, long time.

20

Not Much of a Deal

"The whole school is talking about our booth, thanks to Logan here," Randy told me when I got to school Monday morning, slapping me on the back.

"We're going to make tons of money," Jessica said.

"It will go down in the history books as the best booth ever," Malik bragged.

"Logan, you're a genius," Randy added.

Emily was the only one that didn't act excited. "Leave it to a ratfink to come up with a rodent race," she mumbled.

Just because I was getting all the credit instead of her, she was determined to take away some of the fun. Mom would say that Emily was eating sour grapes, but I wasn't going to let her ruin my mood. Every once in a while I felt a little bad because really, it wasn't my idea at all. It was Grandpa's. But as long as nobody else knew, I wasn't going to worry about it.

Mr. Simon had contacted Mrs. Harrison, and she agreed to help right away. She was even going to provide certificates so winners could save money on cages, bedding, toys, and food at the Tooth and Claw.

The class voted that any money we earned should go to the Humane Society. We wanted to donate a bunch. The middle of the afternoon was the busiest time at the carnival, so that would be the best time to run the races. We organized a way to sell tickets to groups of kids depending on their ages. The top three winners in each race would get their choice of hamsters. Mr. Simon said he had a picnic tent we could use to shelter the cages from the sun. We all signed up to take shifts at the tent to sell tickets and help keep the hamsters calm.

Mr. Simon told us we could write commercials convincing kids how much fun the hamster races would be, and then go into classrooms to act them out. When I told Grandpa, he thought I had just told him he'd won the lottery. "I'll help you, Charlie," he said. "We'll write them together."

I was going to argue, telling Grandpa I didn't need his help, but then I remembered how Mom was trying to convince Dad to send Grandpa away. I figured if he was helping me, he'd be staying out of trouble.

"Sure, Grandpa. We can write the commercials together."

And we did. Side by side at my computer. It turned out that Grandpa was pretty good at coming up with slogans. He also came up with some pretty funny jingles, but there was no way I was going to march into other classrooms and sing them. I didn't tell Grandpa that, though. At least we had fun singing them, until Dad came in and said it was time for bed.

Our class also made posters to hang in the halls and in stores near the school. I had to admit that Emily's posters looked like a pro had done them, but I made sure to hang one that I had done in the front window of the Tooth and Claw.

Every day when I got to the Tooth and Claw, I checked on the hamsters first thing. There were twenty-seven hamsters. Enough for nine races. Mrs. Harrison said she might be able to round up a few more before Saturday.

———

"Looking forward to the carnival this weekend?" Dad asked after dinner on Wednesday.

I was scraping dishes and Dad was putting them in the dishwasher while Mom scrubbed a pan. Grandpa headed downstairs as soon as his plate was empty to watch his television, leaving us to do all the cleanup, which I didn't think was fair at all.

I had planned to spend some of my saved money for the carnival, but since I'd given it to Grandpa for his camera, I was pretty much penniless. "Sort of," I said. "Won't be much fun without any money."

Mom wiped her hands on a towel and turned to face me. "We'll make you a deal," Mom said.

I knew from experience that my parents' deals were never good news. I looked up at Mom as if she had just offered me stewed lizards for dessert.

Dad nodded. "By our calculations, you've collected seven good reports from Mr. Simon. Just three more to go. At this rate, you'll finally have all ten reports next week."

"We know it's been a challenge," Mom said. "We're proud that you've kept trying even after the setbacks you've had. So here's the deal. We'll give you money for the carnival this year."

I looked from Mom to Dad. "Really? You mean it? You'll just give me the money?"

Dad held up his hand. "Not so fast, Logan. Let your mother finish."

Mom smiled. "As I was saying, we'll give you the money, but you have to take your grandfather with you."

"You're kidding, right?" I said. A vision of Grandpa wearing Mom's fuzzy robe popped into my mind, but that was replaced by Grandpa stealing something from the booths. That would get him in trouble, and where my mom was concerned the last thing Grandpa needed was more trouble. I knew staying home would be the safest thing for Grandpa. I had to think fast. "I can't. I'm meeting some kids at the Tooth and Claw and helping take the hamsters to the carnival. I have the first shift at the tent selling tickets and stuff. I won't have time to spend with Grandpa."

"Grandpa can help you," Mom said in a determined voice. "We need you to do this so your father and I can run an errand."

"Can't Grandpa go with you?" I asked.

I noticed Dad was staring at the refrigerator. "Just do as your mother asks, Logan. Besides, this will be the perfect way for you to spend time with your grandfather."

"It's not like I never see him," I told her. "He follows me to the Tooth and Claw every day, and he even does my homework."

"He does what?" Mom snapped, and I couldn't help but notice the look she gave Dad.

"No, no, no," I said in a hurry. "I meant, he *helps* me with my homework."

Mom didn't say another word. Instead she sat and stared at me.

"Mom," I said, "couldn't Grandpa just . . ." And then it hit me.

I knew exactly what my mother and father planned to do while Grandpa was having fun at the school carnival. They were going to look at one of those places where they could take him to live.

I faced Mom and spoke loud and clear. "Grandpa is no trouble," I said. "Of course he can spend the day with me. And you don't have to pay me a single red cent."

21

Girlie Giggles

I wasn't surprised that Grandpa was waiting in front of the Tooth and Claw after school the next day. As long as he wasn't wearing women's clothing, I wasn't going to complain about a single thing he did. I didn't want to give Mom more ammunition.

After a while, he got tired of taking pictures of me cleaning cages. "I think I'll treat myself to an ice-cream cone next door," he said. "I'll meet you in the ice-cream shop after you finish work."

Which was just fine with me.

When I was ready to go home, I found Grandpa next door at the ice-cream shop. "Pistachio used to be my favorite," he was saying to the clerk behind the counter. "Now I'm partial to the fruity flavors. Can't eat anything with nuts. Get under the dentures."

The clerk tried to hide a giggle.

"Don't tell people about your dentures," I whispered when Grandpa said goodbye and turned to leave. "They'll laugh at you."

"There are much worse things than being laughed at," he said for the umpteenth time.

"Like what?" I asked, but I didn't give him a chance to answer, because that's when I noticed it was missing.

"What did you do with it?" I asked.

That panicky look crossed Grandpa's eyes when he wasn't sure what people were talking about. "Do with what?" he asked.

"The camera," I said. "What did you do with your camera?"

Grandpa patted his shirt pockets. He turned in a complete circle and looked on the counter, at the tables, and on chair seats.

The camera wasn't there.

"Maybe you left it at the Tooth and Claw," I said, pulling him out the door.

Mitchell glanced at us with dull eyes when we pushed through the door. "Did anyone turn a camera in?" I asked.

Mitchell shook his head, so Grandpa and I searched the shelves with the cat litter and even shook out the dog beds. It wasn't there.

"When did you have it last?" I asked. "Where have you been? What was the last picture you remember taking?"

But, of course, remembering was the reason for taking the pictures in the first place. Without them, his afternoon turned into a blur. There were no pictures, no sticky notes, nothing left to help him remember. Grandpa took a step away from me and held out shaking hands. "You're asking so many questions, Charlie."

"Think!" I said.

"I'm sorry," Grandpa said. "I . . . I . . . I can't remember. I met you here. I had it then, didn't I?"

Grandpa was looking at me for answers. It hit me then. What it must be like for Grandpa. To realize he should know something, but not being able to dig it up in his brain.

We checked back at the ice-cream shop. We went to the drugstore. We went to the park. We asked everyone along the way. Nobody had seen Grandpa's camera.

"What have I done, Charlie?" Grandpa said as we walked up the sidewalk to our house. With the shorter fall days, it was already getting dark. Dad had turned on the porch light for us. "I lost them. I lost them all. All my memories are gone!"

"It's okay, Grandpa," I told him. "We saved most of the pictures on my computer, so you didn't lose those. Maybe somebody found it and plans to turn it in tomorrow. We'll go back and ask at all the stores after I get out of school."

For once I was right. Somebody did find Grandpa's camera, but I didn't have to wait until after school to find out who it was.

I should have known something was up the moment I saw Emily the next morning. She stood at the top of the steps next to Sharissa and Barbara as if they were a three-headed dragon guarding a cave full of treasure. They were bent over, looking at something in Emily's hands.

"The terrible trio is back together," Malik said as

soon as I walked up. "They've joined forces, and that can only mean one thing for us. Trouble. We have to think of something to ward them off. I wonder if garlic would work on them the same way it works on vampires?"

"Maybe they're just telling knock-knock jokes," I said.

"I don't think so," Malik said. "They keep looking over at us."

He was right. What I heard was even worse. Girlie giggles. A few more kids were trying to look over Emily's shoulders. Emily stood in the middle, smiling. I knew she was right back where she liked to be—center stage.

For the rest of the morning I did my best to ignore Emily. Not the easiest thing to do. By lunch, it was obvious that Emily was planning something and that her evil plan involved me as a victim. I racked my brain, trying to think of what it could be. Tear up my homework? Give me a wedgie? Of course, nothing I thought was even half as bad as what she really planned. I found out at recess. Emily waited until Malik was inside getting a drink. She cornered me by the soccer goal.

"I heard you were looking for something yesterday," she said. "You and your grandfather."

"What do you know about that?" I asked. I narrowed my eyes and gave her my meanest look. She wasn't fazed.

Emily reached in her pocket and pulled out Grandpa's camera. "I bet you were looking for this."

When I grabbed for it, she pulled it away so fast I came up with nothing. I felt like a Rottweiler snapping at empty air.

"Not so fast," she said. "I have a proposition for you."

"No," I said. I didn't need to hear her deal to know it would be bad news for me.

I grabbed for the camera one more time. This time, I snagged it by the strap. The camera slipped off her fingers, and I clutched it for all I was worth. "Aha!" I said. "Got it!"

"I was going to give it back to you anyway," Emily said. "After all, I don't need it anymore."

"What's that supposed to mean?" I asked.

Emily shrugged. "I made backups of all the pictures last night. They're safe and sound on my computer at home."

My mind became a movie of the pictures Grandpa had on his camera. Our neighborhood. The Tooth and Claw. The picture of the dog that could sense seizures. Mom. Dad. Then I remembered. My picture.

"Are you ready to hear me out?" Emily asked.

"I'm listening," I said. My teeth were clenched and my hands curled into fists.

"It's easy. All you have to do is get Malik's backpack and bring it to me," she said. "I plan to solve the mystery of what's inside, once and for all. After that, we'll call it a truce. I leave you alone. You leave me alone."

Her truce would mean nothing to me if I lost Malik as a friend, and that's exactly what would happen if I ratted on him. "What if I say no?"

"Then I'll take that picture. You know the one I'm talking about. The one where you're brushing your teeth? In your *underwear*? And holding a *purse*? And I'll e-mail it to everyone at Dooley Elementary."

"You wouldn't dare," I hissed.

Emily didn't answer. She didn't have to. I knew for a fact that she would send that picture to the president of the United States if only she had his e-mail address.

"Do it tomorrow," she said. "Or else."

22

Wrong Kind of Luck

The dried leaves gave a satisfying crunch with every step we took on Saturday morning. Grandpa was happy. He had his camera again, but he had no idea what it had cost me to get it back.

I should have been happy, too. After all, I only needed one more good report from Mr. Simon. My parents had congratulated me the night before, and Dad said we would pick out my pet next weekend, but I didn't feel the least bit excited, because my mind was a jumble of what-ifs.

What if Emily showed that picture to Sharissa and Barbara?

What if she e-mailed the picture to all the kids in fifth grade?

What if Emily posted the picture on a *Web site*?

My stomach felt like I had swallowed a bowling ball. How in the world could I enjoy cotton candy and popcorn when I had to worry about everyone in the universe seeing my underwear? To make matters worse, I was worried that Mom and Dad might be moving Grandpa's furniture into some distant apartment building.

Grandpa and I stopped by Malik's house on our way to the pet store. Sure enough, Malik's backpack was slung over his left shoulder when he stepped out on the porch. If only I could get him to leave it at home, I'd have a good excuse not to hand it over to Emily.

"You don't want to bring that," I said as matter-of-factly as I could. "It'll only get in the way."

"Are you kidding?" Malik asked. "This has everything in it we need for a full day's adventure. I even have a poncho in case it rains."

"Always prepared," Grandpa said. "Smart thinking."

I glanced up at the sky. The only clouds floating overhead were white and fluffy. "It's not going to rain," I told him.

"You never know," Malik said. "I also have water, snacks, and an extra stash of emergency cash."

Grandpa snapped a picture of Malik and his pack. "Perfect," he said. "I like someone who's prepared for anything."

I gritted my teeth. Maybe if I could get Malik to let me look inside, I could just tell Emily and she'd forget the entire thing. "Let me see."

Malik didn't fall for it. He tapped the bag like he was patting a baby's butt. There was the definite crinkle of cellophane. "Hear that, my friend? It's a jumbo bag of potato chips. I'm willing to share so we don't have to pay extra for chips to go with our hot dogs. That means extra money for games. And for the hamster races."

I had thought about entering the races and trying to win a hamster. After all, I was the fastest runner in the fifth grade, but I had cleaned out enough hamster cages at the Tooth and Claw to last a lifetime. Malik, on the other hand, was determined to win a hamster. Unfortunately, Malik wasn't a fast runner, so he would probably have to enter every race just for a chance to win.

"Why don't you buy a hamster at the Tooth and Claw?" I asked.

"I want our booth to be the biggest money earner this year," Malik answered. "I'm ready to do my part."

I tried a different angle. "Your pack will get in the way. I can see it now. You'll be walking between booths, leaving a path of destruction behind you. Eyes will be blackened. Kids will be flattened. Parents will be crying. It will be terrible. Horrible. A catastrophe. All because you didn't leave your backpack at home."

Malik rolled his eyes. "Don't worry. I'll be careful not to wipe out Dooley's population of kids under the age of five," he argued right back.

Grandpa laughed. "That would make a good story, Charlie. You could call it 'The Path of Destruction.' You should write it, really you should. We'll add it to your computer file of stories when we get home."

It was useless. Malik would not leave his pack behind. I gave up and followed Malik and Grandpa to the Tooth and Claw.

Mrs. Harrison was waiting for us with her van. Grandpa helped carry the cages and other supplies she thought we would need. The hamsters scurried around as if their world were collapsing. I knew just how they felt.

The parking lot and playground had been transformed by the time we arrived. Grandpa stopped as if he'd hit a wall. He stood there, clutching a hamster cage, and looked frantically in all directions. His eyes were wide, like a scared rabbit's. "I don't recognize this place," he said. "What if we get separated?"

I said a few words under my breath. The kind Mom and Dad would ground me for if they knew I used them, but I slowed down so Grandpa wouldn't be left behind.

Mr. Simon had pitched the fifth-grade tent at the end of the playground, and he painted start and finish lines on the grass to show where the races would be. I helped Mrs. Harrison put the hamster cages on the long table under the tent.

"I have to stay for an hour and sell tickets," I told Grandpa. "You can sit there."

Grandpa sat in a folding chair, hidden in shadows. He was quiet, not saying a single word as he watched people hurry by in front of him. I blurred my eyes, trying to imagine what the playground looked like to him as a jumble of colors and people, and I saw how confusing it could be.

All our hard work paid off. Kids were already lining up to buy tickets for the afternoon races. It didn't hurt that Mr. Simon had brought a karaoke machine. The microphone squealed and then sent his voice echoing over the entire neighborhood.

"Welcome to the ninth annual Dooley Carnival," he announced after the feedback died down. "Don't forget to buy your raffle tickets. Someone's going to win that scooter. It might as well be you! Just a dollar a chance! And while you're at it, head over to the fifth-grade Hamster Derby booth and buy your ticket for the races this afternoon."

The hour was over in a snap. Then Malik and I were free to wander around. Well, almost free. Grandpa followed us, sounding like a kid being dragged through the women's underwear department at the mall.

"Wait for me."

"You're going too fast."

"Don't leave me."

"I tell you what," I finally told him as I took the camera out of his hands. I snapped a quick shot of the hamster tent and then pushed the camera back in Grandpa's hands. "If something happens and we get separated, just follow the sound of Mr. Simon's voice over the microphone. That's our tent and I'll meet you there, but I am not going to leave you, okay? So calm down."

I meant it when I said it. Really I did.

More and more people crowded the narrow aisles between booths. The constant chatter of voices and the squealing of Mr. Simon's microphone made it hard to hear. Malik wanted to do one thing, Grandpa another, and he kept taking pictures of everything I did. It was like trying to catch cookie crumbs in a glass of milk.

"Stay here," I told Grandpa. The principal was sitting in the dunking booth, and a group of fourth graders were trying to hit the target that would send her plunging into the water. The smell of roasting hot dogs from a nearby vendor made my stomach growl. "You watch the dunking booth and I'll get us something to eat."

Malik immediately hurried over to the knock-'em-down booth to try his luck at toppling bottles. Grandpa started giving pointers to the fourth graders to help better their aim. I was pretty sure the principal would not appreciate it if my grandfather helped kids knock her into the cold water.

Click. Squeal. The PA boomed over the heads of everyone. "Don't forget the sack races," Mr. Simon's all-too-familiar voice announced. "The first race is for ages six and seven. Ten minutes at the track. Hurry or you'll miss it all! Then visit the fifth-grade booth to get Hamster Derby tickets. They're going fast!"

The hot dog line was so long it snaked around the

booth where people tried to throw Ping-Pong balls into fishbowls. I watched four people lose bunches of money. It was obvious that the hole in the bowl was too small for the Ping-Pong balls, but people kept trying. I knew for a fact it would be cheaper if they bought a fish at the Tooth and Claw.

Finally, I made it to the front of the line. Parents were cheering for the kids in the sack races as I pulled money out of my pocket to pay for the hot dogs. All of a sudden I heard something that made me freeze.

"Charlie? Charlie? Where'd you go, Charlie?"

It was Grandpa. He was threading his way through the crowd, yelling as he got farther and farther away. I grabbed my change, balanced the three hot dogs in my hands, and pushed through the people after him.

"Sheesh," I said, jabbing him with my elbow when I finally caught up. A couple of kids from my class were laughing. Now everyone was going to start calling me Charlie, thanks to Grandpa and his big mouth. "I'm right here. I went to get hot dogs. Remember?"

That look of total confusion flitted across his eyes, and the lines in Grandpa's face seemed deeper when the corners of his mouth turned down. I wanted to be mad at him, but I couldn't. I knew that he hated getting confused even more than I hated being embarrassed. "I told you not to worry, Grandpa," I said. "I won't let you out of my sight."

"I'm sorry," Grandpa said. "There were so many people. I couldn't see you."

"Great," I muttered just loud enough for Malik to hear when he came to grab his hot dog. "Grandpa is having one of his bad days. As if I didn't have other things to worry about."

Blink, blink. Blink. Malik's eyelids fluttered so fast I wondered how he could see. "What do you have to worry about?" he asked. A big blob of mustard had plopped on his sneaker.

I couldn't honestly answer Malik because that meant telling him about my plan to grab his pack, but Malik stood there, blinking at me. I had to say something. Something that would make him forget what I had just said. "I'll tell you what I'm worried about. I'm worried that I'll step up to that knock-'em-down booth and *pow-pow-pow*, I'll knock all the bottles down. Which wouldn't be so bad except look around. See that guy over there—the one leaning against the hot dog stand?"

I had both Malik and Grandpa going. Even Grandpa had stopped chewing his hot dog and looked where I pointed.

"What about him?" Malik asked.

"He's a member of a top-secret band of super-spies. I just saw him pass a bundle of papers to that woman with the sunglasses. This is obviously a rendezvous, and they're trading top secrets. The problem is, once they see me hit that target they'll realize I'm top agent material, and they'll recruit me into their spy ring. I'm not sure I'm ready to be a special agent. I mean, I was sort of looking forward to middle school."

I paused to take a breath. I was so caught up in my own story I had nearly forgotten where I was.

"Oh, good, Charlie," Grandpa said. "Another story. Have you written this one down?"

Malik rolled his eyes for about the nine hundredth time that day. "That was one of your best stories," he said. "Too bad you started by claiming Randy's parents were the spies, though. It's kind of hard to believe that the owners of a shoe repair shop double as agents."

While I had been telling my story, Randy had walked up to his parents. He was trying to get his parents to let him enter the hamster races. His mom was shaking her head so hard I was afraid her earrings were going to fly across the park and put an eye out.

Malik slapped my back. "Besides, for you to hit

that target five times would require tremendous skill and even more luck."

Malik was right about one thing. I needed luck, but obviously, that old saying about being careful what you wish for is true, because I *was* lucky. Only, it wasn't the good kind of luck. It was luck of the Emily variety.

She spotted me just five minutes after Malik headed for the bathroom. It was as if she'd been following us, waiting for the perfect time to make her move.

"Hey, Chuckie-boy," she said right into my ear. I didn't know she was behind me and nearly knocked over a mother trying to wipe snot off her baby's face.

"Chuckie-boy? Who is Chuckie-boy?" Grandpa asked. "I don't know this Chuckie-boy, do I, Charlie?"

Emily took a step back, and her face seemed to go through a hundred expressions before it settled on understanding. Then she looked at me with big eyes. I looked straight back at her, daring her to say something about my grandfather.

"Um . . . I'm sorry . . . I didn't mean to sound rude," Emily stammered.

I couldn't believe it. Emily was actually being nice. "She was just joking," I said, trying to erase the worried look on Grandpa's face. "She means me."

Emily smiled up at Grandpa, and for once it wasn't a snide grin. It was a real smile. "My name is Emily," she said, and I was surprised at how nice and normal she sounded. "It's nice to meet you. Have you gotten any good pictures today?"

Grandpa grasped the camera as if he were gripping a life vest. Then he smiled. "Pictures! Yes. Pictures help me remember. That's what I need. A picture of you and Charlie together!"

"No, Grandpa," I started to argue, but it was too late. Emily moved in so close I could smell peanuts on her breath.

"Smile," she said.

"Leave my grandfather alone," I warned her under my breath.

"I will," Emily answered, and there was nothing malicious in her voice. "Give me a little credit. I'm not going to pick on a nice old man. This is between you and me. I still want that pack. I'll give you an hour. If it's not in my hands by then, I go home and start sending out e-mails with a certain picture attached. The picture that has nothing to do with your grandfather, but everything to do with you."

The spit in my mouth evaporated while Grandpa fired off three shots with his camera.

"I'll be seeing you," Emily said with a wave. "That's a promise."

"More like a threat," I mumbled, because that's exactly what it was.

My brain froze like a fruit smoothie. I was going to have to do it. No way around it. After all, whatever was in Malik's backpack couldn't be as bad as having my underwear picture sent to every kid at Dooley Elementary. I had to figure out a way to lose Grandpa long enough to grab Malik's pack. I was so busy trying to devise the perfect plan that I almost missed my opportunity.

"Logan! Hurry!" Malik shouted.

I shook my head, trying to clear it enough to see why Malik was yelling.

He was tugging on my sleeve, pulling me toward the softball field. "Didn't you hear Mr. Simon's announcement? The first hamster race is starting!" he said. "Tell your grandfather I'll want a picture!"

"Happy to oblige," Grandpa told him as he followed us to the track.

Click. Squeal. The karaoke machine came to life, and Mr. Simon's voice boomed over the playground. "This is what you've all been waiting for. A dollar a race! That's all it takes. All money earned goes right to the Humane Society!"

"Hamsters," Grandpa said. "Mice without the tails. Why don't you enter the races, Charlie? You've been taking care of these critters for weeks. Maybe there's a special one you'd like."

"It's Logan," I said without thinking.

"This is my lucky day," Malik said, turning to me. "Here," he said. "Hold this."

And that's when Malik did the unthinkable—he handed me his backpack.

23

Holding the Bag

I opened my mouth to argue, but not a single word came out. I didn't have time anyway, because Malik was hurrying to get in line for the first race. I was left holding the bag.

It was now or never. "Wait here," I told Grandpa.

"Where are you going?" he asked. I couldn't tell Grandpa the truth, so I did what I did best. Only this time I knew full well it was no story. It was an out-and-out lie.

"Mr. Simon asked me to check on the hamsters."

Grandpa took a step toward me. "But Charlie, you said . . ."

I didn't hear what he was going to say because I had already left him behind. I had to get this over with. Besides, I was only going to be gone for a minute. Just long enough to find Emily and complete the deed.

Timing was everything. I dodged behind a group of kids as they walked by. Then I darted through the tent where the hamsters ran around and around on wheels. I had to squat down behind the hamster display when Mr. Simon walked into the tent to turn up the volume on his karaoke machine. Malik's backpack seemed to drag me backward, its weight heavy and awkward.

As soon as Mr. Simon walked out, I hurried toward the back opening of the tent just as Emily walked past. She grinned at the sight of Malik's backpack dangling from my shoulder.

"Hand it over, Chuckie-boy," she said, reaching for the straps.

"Not until we get a few things straight," I bargained. "First, my name is Logan. From now on, use it. Second, I'm not just handing it over, but if I happen to set it down for a minute and you happen to find it, then I can't help that. If you tell Malik I gave it to you, I'll flat-out deny it until the day I die. Third, once this is over, you leave us all alone. Me, Malik, *and* my grandfather. Forever. Deal?"

Emily squinted her eyes, and I figured she was planning to barter more. I saved her the trouble. "No compromises," I said. "No bargaining. Take it or leave it."

"I would never do anything to hurt your grandfather," she said. "I told you before. This is just between you and me."

It was good to hear her say it, but I didn't really trust her. "Deal?" I repeated.

Emily had been bragging that she would find out what was in Malik's backpack for weeks. If she didn't, she would never hear the end of it. She knew it. I knew it. "Deal," she finally said.

I nodded. "I'm going back to watch the races," I said. "Could be I'll get so interested I'll just happen to set this pack down for a minute. If you know what I mean."

I didn't wait for her to answer. I turned and retraced my steps through the hamster tent. My plan was going off without a hitch . . . until I reached the spot where I'd left Grandpa.

He was gone.

"Have you seen my grandfather?" I asked a group of nearby kids. They looked at me as if I had just sprouted rat's whiskers on the sides of my nose.

Click. Squeal. "On your marks," Mr. Simon yelled over the microphone. "Get set. GO!"

The first race started. People cheered as kids took off, but I couldn't watch. I had to find Grandpa.

I went from group to group, asking the same thing. "Have you seen my grandfather?" I asked. They all shook their heads. No one had seen him.

The more I looked, the more I panicked. There were so many people. Too many booths. He could be anywhere. What if he had wandered away from the carnival and was lost again?

I remembered the way Grandpa looked when I went to get the hot dogs. He wasn't just confused, he was scared. He was having one of his worst days ever, and I had done exactly what I'd promised I wouldn't. I lied and I left him. Alone.

Up until now, my lies were nothing more than tall tales told for a laugh. This lie was different. It meant something. Something serious.

A huge cheer erupted from all around me. The first race was over. I pushed through the crowd, hoping Grandpa was near the finish line so he could take pictures. I got there just in time to see Malik come in dead last.

I turned away from the field and weaved back through the crowd. I glanced at my watch. Grandpa had been missing for nearly fifteen minutes.

I broke free of the crowd, and that's when I ran smack-dab into Emily.

She held out her hand for the backpack. "Where have you been?" she demanded, tugging on the straps.

"Not now," I said. "I can't find my grandfather. He's got this problem with his memory. You wouldn't understand, but I have to find him."

Emily let go of the pack and started looking around. "You're wrong, hamster-breath," she said, and then she totally surprised me when she added, "I know about things like that."

I wondered what she meant when she said she knew about my grandfather's problems, but I didn't have time to think about it.

I shoved her out of the way. "I don't have time for this," I started to tell her. But I didn't get finished, because just then something terrible happened. It was worse than terrible. It was I-could-crawl-in-a-hole-and-never-come-out horrible.

The loudspeaker clunked. A squeal loud enough

to crack teeth cut through the air above the crowd.
Then a loud baritone began singing a slightly off-key
tune.

"Where, oh where has my grandson gone? Oh
where, oh where can he be . . .?"

I knew exactly who belonged to that voice.
Grandpa.

"NO!" I shouted.

The crowd grew quiet. Quiet enough for me to
hear a fifth grader say, "Somebody better find that old
guy and grab the microphone before he has us dancing the hokey-pokey."

"Is that who I think it is?" Emily asked.

"Get out of my way," I snapped, pushing past her.

My day had gone from bad to worse. Thanks to
Grandpa, I was going to be the laughingstock of
Dooley Elementary, but that wasn't what worried
me the most. Now I was worried that Mom and Dad
would find out and ship Grandpa away for good. I
had to stop him before he really caused trouble.

Grandpa finished the song and started singing an
old-time tune. "You ain't nothing but a hound dog!"
he bellowed.

"Hey, Logan," Randy yelled. "Who does your
grandfather think he is? Elvis the Pelvis?"

I felt my face burn as I raced past a bunch of kids

from my class. I hoped Grandpa wasn't dancing like the real Elvis. That would make Mom's mind up for sure about sending Grandpa away.

I darted into the back of the hamster tent. Grandpa was in front of the tent, holding the microphone close to his mouth. A group of people stood in a circle and clapped in time to his off-key singing. Mr. Simon stood a few feet back, not sure what to do. If it had been me, he would have grabbed the mike so fast it would have left burn marks on the palms of my hands. But clearly, my teacher was clueless when it came to disciplining a man who looked old enough to be a caveman. It was up to me to get the microphone, and I had to get it fast. I raced to the front of the tent, picked up the cord, and tugged. Hard.

The microphone flew out of Grandpa's hand. So hard, in fact, it threw Grandpa off balance. Grandpa stumbled. He took three giant steps backward trying to catch his balance. When he did that, he stepped on my sneaker.

"OUCH!" I yelled. I dropped Malik's backpack as I fell back. Unfortunately, I landed right on the table holding the hamster cages.

"NO!" Mr. Simon yelled as the table swayed.

It seemed to happen in slow motion. A leg of the folding table doubled under and the table slanted toward the ground. The cages slid off and the doors sprang open. That's when things sped up again. Hamsters scurried for freedom so fast they were a blur.

"AAAAAHHHHH!" moms screamed.

"AAAAAHHHHH!" dads screamed.

"AAAAAHHHHH!" kids screamed.

I didn't feel like screaming. I wanted to cry.

Grandpa sat on the ground. A hamster ran over his fingers and hid behind his back. His shoulders were slumped, and his forehead creased in deep wrinkles. He refused to look up at me. I had seen my grandfather confused. I had seen him scared. But I had never seen him look so defeated.

I turned away to give him a chance to get back to normal. That's when I saw Emily. She stood right where I had dropped Malik's backpack.

"Mr. Simon is going to cook your butt over a barbecue grill," she said. She hopped over two escaping hamsters and went for Malik's pack.

Mr. Simon was shouting at anyone who would listen. Parents were dancing around, trying to avoid fleeing hamsters. The kids had forgotten about the races and were diving onto the ground. The tent was a wreck.

I took a step toward Emily. "This is your fault," I blurted.

Emily poked me in the chest. "Don't blame this on me," she said as she hoisted the pack off the ground. "I didn't do anything."

I opened my mouth to argue, but then snapped it shut. My day was a disaster. It had all started when I agreed to sell out my best friend and it ended when I abandoned my grandfather. Emily was right. It was me that had made a string of bad decisions, but that didn't mean I couldn't do something now to make it better.

"No!" I said, lunging for the pack. When I did, I tripped over Grandpa's foot. I reached out, trying to catch my balance. Instead, I grabbed a handful of tent. I landed on my knees, bringing the entire tent down with me.

Billowing canvas wrapped around me. A hand clutched my foot. Somebody started pulling me out. "Thanks," I gasped when I finally reached fresh air. I turned to face the person that freed me.

It was Grandpa.

"Doesn't that belong to your best friend?" Grandpa asked as Emily crawled out from under the tent, pulling Malik's backpack with her. "Malik didn't want anyone else to have it. Isn't that why he gave it to you? To protect it? Because he trusted you?"

Grandpa's words stung worse than a chair full of tacks, because I knew he was right.

"Wait," I said, reaching for Malik's pack. "I changed my mind."

Emily looked at me. Then she noticed Grandpa looking at her, and I felt her grip loosen on the pack. "But if I don't find out what's inside, I'll be the laughingstock of school," she said. "It's too late. We had a deal."

She was right. It was too late, because just then I saw Malik. Even worse, Malik saw us.

"What is she talking about?" Malik asked. His eyes darted between my face and my hands, and I realized it looked like I had just handed Emily his backpack. "What deal?"

"It's not what you think," I started to say. Then I shut up because I realized the truth. It *was* exactly what Malik was thinking.

"There you are!" I heard my mother call.

"We've been looking all over for you," Dad added as they rushed through the crowd.

They both looked around at the mess. "What happened?" Dad said. I saw his jaw clenching and realized where I got my habit of gritting my teeth.

When Mr. Simon saw my parents he marched over. There they stood. Malik. Mom and Dad. Mr. Simon. All staring at me.

"Logan, what's going on?" Malik asked.

Dad nodded. "I'd like to hear the answer to that one myself."

"I'll tell you exactly what happened," Mr. Simon said with a voice that sounded very much like a Doberman's growl. "Your son just ruined the carnival!"

24

The Absolute Truth

"It wasn't my fault," I said, but I knew it wouldn't matter how loudly I said the words; they wouldn't be true. Just then a hamster darted over Mom's foot. She jumped back and gave me a look that would freeze hot chocolate.

Malik looked at the pack in Emily's hand. Then he faced me dead-on. "I can't believe it," he said. "Who taught you about friendship? A Tasmanian devil? Genghis Khan? You know something, Logan? Emily was right. You really are a ratfink!"

A million stories flitted through my mind. But I knew that not a single one could make this mess go away. Anything I said would just make me look guilty. Which I was. I stared at the toes of my sneakers and kept my lips sealed. What else could I do? I couldn't look Malik in the eyes.

"I did it."

The words were soft yet strong, but they didn't come from me. They came from Grandpa.

"What?" Mom gasped.

"What?" Mr. Simon said.

"What?" Malik asked.

"I did it," Grandpa said again, only louder. "It was my fault. All of it. I took Malik's pack. I . . . I . . . I got confused. I thought it belonged to this young lady. Charlie . . . I mean Logan . . . was trying to get it back. I didn't realize what he was doing and I made a mistake and knocked over the tables. And the tent. I did it all. It was me. Charlie . . . I mean Logan . . . was trying to fix what I messed up." And then Grandpa looked my mother straight in the eyes and said, "You know how I am. I'm always making a mess of things."

Mom shot a look at Dad. I knew that look. It was her I-told-you-so look.

I was king of the whoppers, but even this one took

me by surprise. Thanks to Grandpa's lie, I could walk away from this mess with everything I wanted. Malik would still be my best friend. I wouldn't be in trouble with Mr. Simon. I'd get the pet of my choice.

But that's not all that would happen.

If I let Grandpa take the blame, Mom would have the ammunition she needed to tuck Grandpa safely away in one of the places they had gone to see.

Grandpa might not remember my name all the time. He might forget his way home. He might even do things that were downright embarrassing. But Grandpa also helped me with my homework. He liked to hear my stories, and he was the one person willing to listen to my side of things. Now he had proven that he would do anything for me. He would never betray my trust.

That's when I knew the absolute, honest-to-goodness truth. If I let Grandpa take the blame, it would make me the biggest ratfink ever.

"It's not true," I said.

Grandpa reached out and put a hand on my shoulder. It was firm and warm. "Leave it be," he said softly.

I shook my head. "No," I told Grandpa. "I can't."

Then I told the truth. The whole truth, and nothing but the truth. When I got to the part about Emily having my picture, Malik gasped. "She has a picture?" he asked. "Of you? In your underwear?" He said the last word in a whisper.

Grandpa looked at the camera dangling from his fingers. "I didn't mean for anything like that to happen," he said. "I just wanted to remember you."

"I know, Grandpa," I told him. "It isn't your fault. It's mine. All mine."

"Why didn't you tell us?" Mom asked.

"I tried," I said.

Dad nodded. "Yes, you did. I'm sorry, Logan. I should've listened."

Mom looked at Dad. Dad looked at Grandpa. Mr. Simon looked at us all. Finally, Malik met my eyes.

"It's Emily's fault, too," Malik added.

I looked at Emily, wanting to rat her out. She gave me that same scared look that she had given me on the first day of school when she worried about walking into a room full of strangers, and for some reason that reminded me of when Grandpa had pretended to be a chicken in the middle of the park. I suddenly understood what Grandpa had been trying to tell me. Sometimes people do pretty weird things when they find themselves the center of attention.

I shook my head. "It's not Emily's fault. She was

just trying to fit into a new school. I should have told Emily no, but I didn't."

The look Emily gave me was like the one Grandpa always had when he suddenly realized where he was or what he was supposed to be doing. It was the look of relief.

And then I did what I should have done a long time ago. I apologized to Malik.

"I believe you," Malik said, suddenly holding the pack out toward me. "Go ahead. Give it to her. If you don't, she might really send out that picture. A seismograph wouldn't be able to register the laughing."

I looked at the pack in Malik's outstretched hand. It would be so easy. Take it, hand it over to Emily. Be done with everything. But Malik would always know that I had sold him out just to keep from being embarrassed. What was worse, I would know. And unlike Grandpa, I wouldn't be able to forget.

I shrugged. "So what if they laugh?" I asked. Then I looked at Grandpa and said the words I'd heard so often. "There are worse things than being laughed at. Like losing my best friends—both of them."

It was then that I knew the absolute truth.

I *was* like my grandfather. And it wasn't such a bad thing after all.

25

Epilogue

This is the part where I should say I lived happily ever after, but that would be another whopper, and I don't tell those anymore. Now I write them down instead. Grandpa helped me set up files on my computer for all my writing. There I can make anything happen, but in real life things don't always turn out exactly the way you want them to.

At least my picture was never sent over the computer to anyone's e-mail, because Emily lost all her

computer privileges after Mr. Simon had a confer-
ence with her parents. She still bugs me every chance
she gets. She wouldn't be Emily if she didn't, but it
really isn't so bad. Emily's right about one thing. She
is smart. Smart enough to know that we both messed
up.

I learned to live with it. So did she.

I never found out what was in Malik's backpack.
He offered to show me one night when he was sleep-
ing over. I thought long and hard about it. I'd wanted
to know what was inside for years. Plus, knowing
what was inside would give me something to lord over
Emily. On the other hand, it was sort of fun having
a mystery at Dooley Elementary. Besides, if Malik
wanted to keep it to himself, that was his business. It
meant a lot, though, that he offered.

I knew it meant just as much to him that I de-
clined.

The mystery of what was in his backpack did give
me an idea for a story. In fact, Grandpa is helping me
write it. Come to find out, he and I have something in
common. We're both pretty good at writing stories. I
let Malik read what we have so far. He says it's good
enough to be made into a book. Who knows? Maybe
someday it will be. I'm even thinking about asking

Emily to illustrate it, but I'll have to think about it a lot longer to be sure.

I didn't get the pet I had earned. It was pretty much understood that conspiring to betray my best friend and ruining the school carnival voided anything I had earned during those two weeks. I get to be around animals, though, because Mrs. Harrison said I could keep working at the Tooth and Claw for as long as I wanted.

That isn't all.

Right before Thanksgiving, I told my parents about an idea I had. And they listened. Really listened. They do that a lot now.

I showed them an article all about it. Mom and Dad sat, shoulder to shoulder, and read the article. I almost forgot to breathe as I waited for them to decide. Finally, they put the magazine down and looked right into my eyes.

Dad talked first: Are you sure, Logan? It would be very expensive.

Then it was Mom's turn: It would be a big responsibility.

I was ready with my answer: It's the perfect gift. I'll give up my allowance for the next five years to do it.

"I'll do whatever it takes to make it work," I added, and I meant it. Still do.

Mom looked at Dad. Dad looked at Mom. Then they both nodded.

The next week Dad asked Mrs. Harrison to help, and together we found the perfect one. Two days before Christmas, we presented Grandpa with his present.

Her name is Sadie, and she's been specially trained as a companion dog for someone just like Grandpa. Now we don't have to worry about him getting lost. Sadie always leads him right back to our house. That means Grandpa won't have to move anywhere. At least not for a long, long time.

So even though I never got a pet of my own, it's okay. Grandpa and I take Sadie for long walks. Together.

And I don't care at all who happens to see us.